Hood Love
By: Leondra LeRae

D0104924

DEDICATION:

To Stephen Walker, I love you so much and I miss you!! Rest Peacefully
To my grandparents Avis and Leonard Williams, I love you and miss you terribly; I hope you guys continue to Rest in Paradise!

To everyone who doubted and didn't believe in me and every HATER; THIS IS FOR YOU!

ACKNOWLEDGEMENTS:

First and foremost, I would like to thank my Heavenly Father God! Thank you for giving me the gift of writing! I am nothing without You – You pushed me and now here I am releasing my first ever book!!! Thank You Thank You Thank You I Love You!!!

My paternal grandparents, Avis and Leonard, I wish you guys were here to watch me shine! I know you guys would have been proud. I love you guys and I miss you both terribly! May you continue to Rest in Paradise.

My maternal grandparents, Joan and Joseph, I love you both. Never forget it. I'm so glad to have you guys and I wouldn't trade you for the world!

Stephen Walker, words can't express the hurt and sadness that I feel for you leaving me so suddenly. You were a wonderful father to my siblings and companion to my mother. You were supposed to witness my success first hand with me but God needed you first. I can't believe you're really gone, it seems so unreal. I will miss the times we argued like husband and wife hence the nicknames "husband and wife", long talks, cries and all the shit talking you did. You will forever be my husband and no one can take your place! I love you always and forever. Rest in Paradise my love!

To my father, Leonard, I love you Daddy! Thank you for always being here for me, always believing in me, never turning your back on me, and allowing me to steal your computer for hours at a time so I can get this done! Although you never knew the reason I always took your laptop! Lol I love you dad and I promise to make you proud of me.

To my mom, Charlotte, I love you! Thank you for pushing me into doing this. You were the first one to begin reading this and telling me it was hot and that I should continue. You gave me the confidence I needed to get through this. I appreciate you much!

My cousin Quia, ain't too much to say because you already know the deal! I love you girlie, thanks for all the talks, cries, laughs; everything! The wait is finally over and now 'Hood Love' is complete!

My Uncle Matt aka Uncle Suge, you are something else, you've always been there to guide me even when I just so happen to fall off the right path. I'll let you have your credit for the title if that is what will make you happy although we both know the truth, lol. I love you Unc!

My siblings; Adryan, Rayna, Leonard III, Mattie, Marquis & Stephanie, I love you all equally and unconditionally! All six of you give me the strength to go on every day and want better for myself and you guys! We all are going places in our lives and I can't wait to see where we end up!

My nephew/godson Armani, auntie loves you to death! Never ever forget it or question it!

Ta'Naz, God'Mommy loves you baby!

My unborn nephew, I can't wait to meet you, I love you!

My cousins, aunts, uncles, I love you all. I can't name everyone or I would be here forever. But just know, I love and appreciate every last one of you guys.

My best friends Kelly, Diane and Antwon, I love you all to death! I can't imagine life without yall!

Ms. Lekecia Bri'Monae! Thank you Ms. Lady! You're the one who really pushed me by putting that damn deadline on me, but I'm so glad you did because if you didn't, who knows when this would have been done! I'm glad you enjoyed it as much as you did! Lol this will be one of a few & I expect you to be around every step of the way, Love you!

Ms. Gabrielle GotemHatin Dotson! Girl I don't even KNOW where to begin! You've been by my side thru this since the beginning! Test reading for me every couple of chapters, the whole nine, I can't thank you enough, but I can say, I look forward to working with you & I know I got you here for a while, if not for good. Thanks for everything Ma! Love you!

Nai Loving E Sawyer – man oh man, thanks girlie, for everything you've done! Down to the long random talks lol, I see plenty more coming soon, love you mama

Hadiya Mcduffie, girl you are my strength!! I see all you post and what you go through, you are my inspiration!! You are a beautiful strong woman & I promise to always be here for you; you will always have a friend in me forever and a day, I LOVE YOU MA!!!!

My SECRET SOCIETY! Tamika, Shae, Coco, and Hassan, lol I love yall crazy asses! Always & forever!

Ms. Tajana Sutton, thank you for letting me use your group as a venting place as well as a promoting station! I appreciate it more than you could ever imagine and I can't thank you enough! I LOVE YOU!

David Weaver, where do I begin with your crazy behind? Thanks for everything; thanks for giving me a second family and another place I can call my home away from home; I love you!

SHOUTOUT TO MY BANKROLL SQUAD FAMILY! I LOVE YALL!!!

SHOUTOUT TO EVERYONE IN THE TAJANA SUTTON FAN GROUP! THANK YALL FOR ALL THE LOVE & SUPPORT, IT TRULY MEANS EVERYTHING!

MY BRI'MONAE'S WORLD FAMILY; YALL MADE ME LAUGH WHEN I DIDN'T EVEN FEEL LIKE SMILING, I LOVE YALL CRAZY ASSES!

MY MC FAMILY! Jass, Cedes, Danni, Tiff, Licia, Dwinique, Kiy, Cam, Keem, Zo, Ty, and anyone else; I love yall! Yall are my escape from reality when things get tough.

If I missed anyone in these acknowledgments, PLEASE, PLEASE, PLEASE, charge it to my head & not to my heart!

I hope ya'll enjoy reading this as much as I enjoyed writing it! I now present to you
"HOOD LOVE"

Peace,
Leondra LeRae

Prologue

"What the fuck was that?" Jonnae thought and jumped up as the heard the front door of her house being kicked in. Capo had always told her to be prepared for a day such as this. She then remembered, Capo didn't move, so she glanced to the opposite side of the bed and realized he wasn't there. "Where the fuck did he go?" she thought to herself. Her instincts told her things were going to get ugly if she didn't do something quick. She heard the intruders messing up the living room and kitchen. She quickly locked the bulletproof bedroom door which automatically caused a projection screen to drop and the cameras that were placed in the house to show the footage of the living room and kitchen. It brought tears to her eyes to see the living room and kitchen a total mess.

She got herself together and ran to Capo's closet, which held the door to a smaller room that contained emergency guns, clothes, money, drugs and anything else that could be needed. This room also had TVs that showed every room in the house. She constantly wondered, "Where the fuck is Capo?" As she glanced back to the television screens, she realized that the intruders were no longer in the living room and kitchen but they were heading up the stairs in her direction.

She threw on an all-black sweat suit and a pair of black tennis shoes as fast as she could. She grabbed her emergency hand bag that she kept in the hidden room and started throwing all the stacks of money and a few guns in the bag. She looked back at the screens again and realized the intruders were heading towards the bedroom door. She started panicking but tried to remain under control because if she panicked, it could cause her life. She ran to the other door in her closet, which led to a tile in the garage ceiling. She heard the bedroom door come crashing down. Once she dropped onto the garage floor as quickly and quietly as possible, she hoped she had enough time to get the garage door open and flee the house before the intruders made it back downstairs.

She quickly decided on taking Capo's Corvette over the Range Rover, the seven series Beemer and the C-class Mercedes. She quickly pressed the button on the car remote to open the garage door. That was the one thing she hated about the house, the garage door made so much noise as it opened and moved slow. The Corvette was started and the doors were locked. She felt a little safer in the cars because all of them cars were bulletproof all around.

As soon as the garage door opened enough for the Corvette to slide out, the door that separated the house from the garage went flying open. Jonnae stomped on the gas pedal as she glanced in her review mirror into a pair of eyes she once told herself she would never forget. She couldn't believe the person who once owned her heart and soul was the same person who ransacked her home.

Chapter 1

1 year earlier:

I think I'm ready, been locked up in the house way too long, it's time to get it, cause once again he's out doing wrong. Jonnae sang along to Beyoncé's Freakum Dress as she prepared her make up for prom. It was her junior prom and her boyfriend's senior prom. Jonnae and her boyfriend Chink had been together since Jonnae's freshman year of high school. From the moment she laid eyes on him, she knew she had to have him. He was her first love as well as the man who she lost her virginity too. She worshipped the ground that Chink walked on and didn't think he could do any wrong, especially in her eyes.

Of course there were people who envied the couple. Everyone knew that Jonnae was Chink's leading lady. He was a known hustler. He wasn't rich, but he made enough to keep Jonnae laced in the up-to-date gear that was out. Just about every Jordan that came out, Jonnae had. If she walked into the store and seen something she wanted, if she gave Chink the look, all he did was peal the cash off the top. He kept his dealings low key to stay off the radar of the police.

Chink and Jonnae met when he approached her during the second week of school as he seen her standing at her locker talking to her friend Mya. He waited until the conversation was over and as Jonnae started walking away, Chink approached her.

"Hey ma, wait up for a second." Chink called.

Jonnae stopped and turned around to see who was trying to get her attention. When she saw who it was, her stomach instantly had butterflies floating around. Throughout the two weeks she had been in high school, she heard enough about Chink. She knew all the girls wanted him, and hell who could blame them. The man was gorgeous. He was the skin complexion of Trey Songz. He kept a low haircut that had so many waves; people could probably get sick just looking at them. Okay maybe not that serious but Chink's waves were nice. His eyes were a dreamy dark brown. He had a nice set of lips; not as big as Jay-Z but they were coming in close second.

Jonnae was at a complete loss for words.

"Glad I could catch you before you left."

Jonnae blushed, "well you have my attention so what's up?"

"Let's save all the talking for the phone, slide me your number and I'll call you tonight." Chink responded.

Jonnae smiled, "How about you give me your number and I'll call you. At least then I can call when I'm ready."

Chink liked her already. She was feisty and he didn't mind it one bit. He knew that she was a freshman and he also knew that she lived with her mother and older brother who happened to be as protective as a father although he was only older than Jonnae by three years. Chink knew about Jonnae's brother, whose name was Jonathan, but was known as Boog. Boog was a known hustler in the area and he was known for laying a nigga on his back, especially when it came down to Jonnae. Even Boog's two best friends Chiefy and KB treated Jonnae as their little sister. Anyone who fucked with Jonnae was asking for a death wish.

Chink laughed as he took Jonnae's Blackberry and punched in his number. "First things first, we're gonna upgrade this phone. Don't nobody walk around with a crackberry anymore."

Jonnae burst into laughter, "How you gonna ask me for my number then make fun of the kind of phone I have? You have some nerve boy." They both continued laughing. Jonnae checked the time on her phone screen,

"Look I gotta go, either my brother or one of his two friends are outside waiting for me. I'll give you a call." Jonnae turned and walked away before Chink could answer.

"I sure hope so ma, I really hope so." Chink mumbled to himself before heading home.

That was the beginning of Jonnae and Chink and now two years later, here they were still thick as thieves.

Chapter 2

As Jonnae finished the touches of her make-up and unpinned her curls, her song she always dedicated to Chink bumped through the speakers of her iHome. *Let me cater to you, cause baby this is your day, do anything for my man, baby you blow me away, I got your slippers, your dinner, your desert, and so much more.* Jonnae grabbed her roller brushed and used it as a microphone as she sang along to the Destiny's Child hit.

Her mother peeked through the door, "Nae, you sound like a howling wolf. Please let the girls sing their songs before you kill it and no one ever wants to hear it again." Her mother burst into laughter.

"Why you such a hater? Mad cuz I sing better than you." Jonnae responded, chuckling.

"Girl please, only in the shower could you sound better than me." They shared a laugh

"I'm gonna let you finish getting dressed so you're not late. I'll call you when Chink gets here." Her mom stated as she walked out the door.

Twenty minutes later, Jonnae finished putting her prom dress on. She bought the dress three months prior because she knew she had to have it. Because she ordered it online and from overseas, she would most likely be the only one at the prom with this exact dress. It was a long purple, one strap dress. Her entire left side was showing and the dip stopped right before her ass. The back had straps going across completely covered in rhinestones. The dress alone cost close to four hundred dollars, not including the shoes and accessories. Chink made it well known that his woman only wore the best. For the prom, between Chink and Jonnae's mom, she had spent close to a stack for everything. She definitely wanted this to be a night to remember.

Jonnae happened to be walking by her window, when she looked out and noticed Chink standing outside on the phone in a heated argument. Damn, even when he is mad, he looks fine as hell. She had to pry her eyes away from the window or else she would have been climbing back in the shower. As she gave herself a look over again In her full body mirror, she heard her mom yelling for her.

"Jonnae, Chink is here; hurry up before you're late."

She took a deep breath before she walked out of her room. She slowly descended the stairs as she came face to face with the man she loved.

"Wow, ma, you look absolutely gorgeous." Chink was at a loss for words. Jonnae was beautiful regardless, but she looked absolutely stunning in the dress. He had never seen the dress before this day. She made it perfectly clear that she wanted it to be a surprise and the only detail she would give him was the color of it.

Jonnae's mom couldn't hold back the tears of joy. She had seen the dress prior, but this was the first time she saw it on Jonnae. "Look at my baby girl. You look amazing. I wish your brother was here to see this, he would be so proud."

Jonnae hated when her mom brought up her brother. She missed him terribly. He had gotten caught selling to an undercover and was now serving a three year bid behind it. He was two years in and Jonnae and Boog were counting down the months until he came home. Jonnae wrote Boog often and was at every visit.

"Ma stop because if you make me cry and ruin my makeup, it's gonna be a problem." Jonnae smiled away the tears that were threatening to fall from her eyes.

Chink looked flawless in his suit. The purple of the dress was the same exact purple as the one in Chink's tie and handkerchief. Chink placed the corsage on Jonnae's wrist and started posing for pictures as her mother was snapping pictures left and right, whether the couple was ready or not. After thirty minutes of taking pictures, the couple finally left. Jonnae couldn't wait to get to the prom and see all her friends, especially Shakeisha. Shakeisha kept her dress a surprise from everyone. She didn't want to chance anything by having someone else show up to prom with her dress on.

This was Jonnae's best day of her life. Or so she thought. Jonnae and Chink showed up at prom and as always, eyes of envy were staring at them. As they walked through the ballroom, stares were coming from everywhere. Jonnae spotted her girls standing near each other waiting for her and Chink. Jonnae held onto Chink's hand and started walking over to her girls and their dates until she felt Chink being pulled in another direction.

Jonnae turned around in time to see one of the many chicks who wanted Chink all in his face.

"So you couldn't take me to prom because you showed up with this hoochie?" Tayla stated.

Jonnae couldn't believe the drama starting already and she just walked through the door. She wanted to enjoy one drama free night. She didn't want to be approached about anything that Chink may have done. She wanted this to be the perfect night.

"Whoa shawty; you really need to chill. I don't know what made you think I would have taken anyone else to prom except for my wife. What kinda shit you smoking?' Chink replied.

Jonnae suppressed her laugh, until reality kicked in that this trick called her a hoochie.

"Hold up hoe, who you calling a hoochie? Don't be mad because I got what you want." Jonnae said.

At that time, Jonnae's girls left their dates and headed towards the commotion.

Chink pulled Jonnae back, "Chill ma, she knows the deal, I don't even know why she's even tryna start some shit."

Jonnae turned to walk away. She wasn't gonna let some hood rat ruin what was supposed to be the best day of her life. She danced with her girls and partied the night away.

She took her prom picture with Chink, and danced until her feet hurt. Jonnae figured she would sit down for a few songs and cool off. That was until the DJ started playing slow jams. Slow jams were Jonnae's weakness. Soon as she heard the beat of "*All My Life*" by K-Ci and JoJo, she scanned the room for Chink. She was getting annoyed that she couldn't find him until she felt breath on her neck.

"You mind if I have this dance beautiful?" Chink whispered in Jonnae's ear.

She blushed, "I wouldn't want to share this dance with anyone else."

Chink led Jonnae to the dance floor, wrapped his arms around her waist and swayed side to side with the beat of the song.

As they danced, Chink started singing the words as he looked into Jonnae's eyes.

You're all that I ever known, when you smile, your face glows, you picked me up when I was down, and I hope that you feel the same way too, yes I pray that you do love me too. All my life, I prayed for someone like you, and I thank God that I, that I finally found you. Jonnae's heart melted as Chink sang the words she knew he meant.

"I love you Jonnae Myeisha Carter."

Jonnae smiled, "And I love you too Erick Montrell Jackson."

The DJ called last song and all the couples headed out to the dance floor as the beat of "*Meeting in my Bedroom*" by Silk began to play.

"I know there will be a lot of people getting their freak on tonight, just be smart and use Trojan. Spend $2 on a box of condoms rather than thousands on a baby. Hope y'all enjoyed yourself because I know damn sure I did. Last song of the night and this goes out to all the couples who were able to share this night together. Special shout out to my man Chink and his shorty Jonnae, I see you my dude."

Chink threw up a quick piece sign to the DJ as he shared the last dance with the woman he wanted to spend the rest of his life with. Jonnae rested her head on Chink's chest and Chink rested his chin on her head.

He leaned down and whispered, "*There's a meeting in my bedroom, so girl please don't be late.*"

Jonnae chuckled. She truly enjoyed herself and felt happy.

Chapter 3

Jonnae and Chink were walking out the door when Tayla felt the need to approach them again.

"Chink we need to talk." Tayla declared

Chink sucked his teeth, "Man we ain't got shit to talk about Tayla, damn. Leave me the hell alone. What's so hard about you doing that?"

Jonnae snickered, "*If it's one thing I can't stand it's a thirsty bitch, and that's exactly what this hoe is. Thirsty!*"

"I don't know what your ass is snickering at. That's the problem with ya dumb ass now, you think you have the best relationship out here and you think ya man does no wrong. Best believe, this nigga ain't an angel. He gets around, been around to me too. Only thing is, I'm not gonna sit here and let the nigga play me like he does every other bitch."

Jonnae wouldn't allow Tayla to see her anger and hurt that her words caused. Jonnae took one step towards Tayla, "Let me tell ya ratchet ass something, this right here," she pointed to Chink, "belongs to me. You say he gets around, but every muthafuckin night, he comes home to me. You're just like every other hood rat around this muthafucka, always bragging about having the next bitches man not realizing it makes you look like a dumb fuck. You're fuckin' retarded; you think you were doing something major by saying what you just said? No dummy, you made yourself look like an idiot because now everyone knows how obsessed you are over a nigga that doesn't want ya loose pussy ass. Its bitches like you that cause me not to trust others. You grimy as fuck Tayla, and I'll tell you what, because I don't wanna ruin this $400 dress that MY man paid for, I'm not gonna lay ya ass out like I want too. Next time, I won't hesitate. Now remember that the next time you wanna talk shit. Fuckin' ratchet ass bitch!

Jonnae walked away, head held high, holding in every emotion that she felt. She wanted so badly to cry, because she felt like an idiot. Here she was again, protecting her man and their relationship when everything Tayla said was most likely true. It just killed her to believe it. She knew Chink wasn't an angel, she just strongly believed he wasn't like other niggas out on the streets.

She climbed in the Hummer limo that was waiting outside for her and Chink, she completely broke down. She was sick and tired of fighting chicks over Chink. She loved him with every fiber of her being, but she couldn't take any more of his infidelities. It hurt too much to deal with it. Chink got in the limo and noticed Jonnae's tear stained face.

"What's wrong bae? Why you crying?" Jonnae stared into Chink's beautiful eyes and realized again why she was so deeply in love with this man who constantly hurt her.

She sighed, "I just want this night to end. Once again, I get embarrassed in public because your dick can't seem to stay in your pants. Once again, I'm out here ready to pound a bitches face in because she's telling me she slept with my man. Once again, I'm a fool for your love. I'm tired Erick, I really am. This was supposed to be the best night of my life, but nope, it just can't happen. Jonnae can't go anywhere without being approached about her man."

Chink knew Jonnae was serious because that was the only time she used his real name; when she was truly hurt or pissed.

Chink slid closer to her and wiped away Jonnae's tears. "Ma I promise you, I never touched that girl. She's a hoe, why would I even look her way? I.."

Jonnae cut him off, "maybe not her, but what about the other girls? I know damn well you done screwed other girls while we've been together and I know there are a few from school. I'm not an idiot, I just play blind eye to it all, because I don't wanna believe that my man is just like these other niggas out here. I give you everything and anything you ask and it still isn't enough for you. What else am I supposed to do?" Jonnae couldn't stop the tears from falling. She truly was hurt.

The limo pulled up in front of her house. All the lights were off so she knew her mother was sleeping. They both stepped out of the limo and walked up the stairs to her door. Jonnae turned to face Chink before she opened the door.

"I wanna be alone tonight Chink. I need to clear my head." She saw the disappointment sweep across his face.

"Nae really? I can't believe you're letting what this bitch said get to you. I told you I never touched that broad! Why are you letting this ruin our night? Please, let's just go to your room and go to bed." Jonnae wasn't in the mood to argue, she wanted to slide the dress off, put on her pajamas and go to bed.

She unlocked her door and made her way to her room with Chink on her trail. Jonnae took her dress off, laid it across her desk chair, threw on one of Chink's t-shirts and a pair of his boxers and headed to the bathroom to wipe the makeup off her face. When she returned, Chink was climbing into the bed with his basketball shorts and wife beater. Jonnae snuggled up next to him and silently cried herself to sleep. She knew if Chink continued with his way, this would be the end of their relationship.

Chapter 4

Jonnae woke up the next morning to the sound of vibration. She quickly grabbed her phone to stop the noise when she realized, it wasn't her phone. She looked up and noticed Chink's phone sitting on her desk. She grabbed it and she noticed the text message icon on the screen. *Why is Tayla texting him? Didn't she get the concept last night? Let's see what this bitch wants now!* Jonnae thought. She opened the message: "***I dnt appreciate tha way u tried to play me last nite jus cuz u was around tht bitch, she's a dum ass if she thinks ya faithful, ya a fuckin dog and I cnt wait until her blind ass sees that***" Jonnae's face turned into a scowl after reading that message.

"Chink wake ya ass up." Jonnae screamed. She was tired and fed up of dealing with his bullshit.

"Damn bae, what's the matter" he questioned.

Jonnae threw his phone at him. "Call ya bitch and tell her I said stop texting you before she ends up with her fuckin face bashed in and I'm not playing." Jonnae walked out the room towards the bathroom.

"It's too early in the morning to be dealing with this bullshit man." Chink checked his phone and seen the open message. 'This bitch ain't gonna be happy until Jonnae molly whops her ass." Chink responded to the message. "*aye shortie, stop hittin me up man, I dnt want ya ratchet ass and I told you that from fuckin jump, u tried hittin on me and I set ya ass str8, u insist on fuckin wit me but u won't be happy until wifey whoops ya ass, dnt say I didn't warn u, ill holla*" he sent the message and hoped it would be the last he heard from Tayla.

He got out of bed and headed to the bathroom to release his bladder. He walked in as Jonnae was brushing her teeth. He took a piss and washed his hands. He then wrapped his arms around Jonnae's waist and looked in the mirror at their reflection. They truly were picture perfect. Chink never thought he could love any other woman besides his mother but his love for Jonnae ran deeper than words could express. He couldn't figure out why he couldn't help but to have a girl on the side when he had all he needed standing right in front of his face. He made a promise to start doing right by Jonnae. This was his last year of high school and he would be graduating in five weeks. He would have never made it this far without her.

Jonnae sucked her teeth, removed his arms and walked away. Chink knew he was on the verge of losing her and he couldn't nor did he want to deal with the thought of that.

"Jonnae what's wrong? You won't even talk to me, how am I supposed to be able to fix this if I don't know what's wrong?" Chink begged

Jonnae spun around, "If you learned to keep your dick in ya pants, we wouldn't have anything to be tryna fix now would we?" He stood there dumbfounded. "Yeah I thought so. Just go, Chink. I don't wanna argue today, I'll call you later." Jonnae walked over to her room. Her heart ached badly. She never in a million years thought she would be going through this with Chink. She thought he was her soul mate. The one she would spend her life with. With the recent events that happened, she highly doubted they would last to the end of the school year. Jonnae threw herself across the bed as silent tears slid down her cheeks. She was tired of crying. The only way to fix the situation she was in was to drop the problem; and the problem was Chink! He grabbed a t-shirt that he knew he left at Jonnae's, threw on his Jordan flip flops and walked out the door to his car. He wasn't the type to pray, but as he left her house, he prayed to God that he wouldn't lose Jonnae behind his ways. He knew he needed to change, but he didn't know how too.

Jonnae got dressed, called Shakeisha and headed to her house. As she made her way to Shakeisha her phone rang. A number she didn't recognize showed up on her screen. She was hesitant to answer but she did anyway.

"Hello."

"Hi, I'm looking for Jonnae," a soft voice responded.

"This is her, who's this?" Jonnae questioned

"My name is Lena, you may or may not know about me, but I know a little about you. I know you've been dating Chink for the past almost three years, I know y'all go to school together, but I've been sleeping with him for the past six months and I'm three months pregnant."

Jonnae felt her heart race as this Lena girl told her she was pregnant by her man. Her Chink, her first love, her everything. She felt her world crash and burn right at her feet.

"Wait a second, who did you say you was?" Jonnae was almost speechless; her voice was caught in her throat.

"I'm Lena, I would say ask Chink about me, but like all other niggas, he's just gonna deny it. I wanted you to hear about this from and not from some gossip around the street." Jonnae gained a little respect for Lena for being the one to confront her with this situation.

Jonnae couldn't believe her ears, "This is fuckin crazy, if it ain't one thing with this nigga; it's another. Hey can I call you back at this number?" Jonnae had to get off the phone and get to Shakeisha's house quick before she broke down.

"Sure; and I want you to know that I am sorry about this. I didn't know about you until I already found out I was pregnant. That's when he decided to tell me that I needed to have an abortion because he had a wifey that he has been with for almost three years and that he wasn't trying to lose her," Lena stated.

Jonnae couldn't believe what she was hearing. This was truly the icing on the cake. She couldn't take it anymore.

"I don't blame you, well I do, but I don't put it past Chink to say some of the shit you said that he said. Let me give you a call a little later." Jonnae hung up before Lena could even respond.

She had just got to Shakeisha house as she hung up. She rang the doorbell wanting Shakeisha to hurry up and open the door. She was fighting to hold back the tears. Soon as Shakeisha opened the door, Jonnae lost it.

"I can't take this anymore Keisha, I really can't," Jonnae sobbed. Shakeisha didn't even have to ask what she was talking about because she already knew.

She let Jonnae cry; she knew she needed to do so in order to let go of all her emotions.

"Let's go Nae, we're gonna walk to the store. You need fresh air." Shakeisha expressed.

Jonnae and Shakeisha were walking down the street to the store. Jonnae was ranting to Shakeisha how she was sick of Chink and his cheating ways. Shakeisha heard it all before and hoped and prayed that Jonnae meant it truly this time.

"Damn, Keisha, I've been dealing with this nigga for so long, he's all I know. But I'm tired of fighting bitches over him. Every time a bitch talk greasy about that nigga, I'm right there pounding her face in. That shits getting old man." Jonnae stated.

"Nae, I've been telling you this for months to leave that nigga alone. You've been fighting bitches over that nigga since the beginning. Chink wasn't shit when you met him and over the years, he got worse. I'm tired of watching you beat bitches asses. Don't get me wrong, you definitely can handle your own, but damn, you wanna be fighting bitches forever?"

Jonnae sighed, "Keisha, this shit is annoying. Oh, before I forget, on my way over to your house, I got a call from some chick named Lena claiming that she's pregnant by Chink and she knew nothing about me and had she known she would have never even started fuckin with him. That just fucked my whole entire head up."

Shakeisha stopped dead in her tracks, "Did you say a bitch named Lena? Knocked up by Chink?"

Jonnae nodded.

"Oh hell no; wait let's get our shit from the store and we'll finish this on the way back."

Chapter 5

Jonnae and Shakeisha quickly grabbed two Arizona Ice Teas, paid and were heading out the door when someone walked in.

Jonnae froze in her place not because she knew the man, but because he was the finest man she ever seen.

Shakeisha turned to walk out the door, "so as I was saying about that bitch Lena..." She walked dead into Jonnae. She followed Jonnae's eyes, "Damn he's fine!"

All Jonnae could do was nod. This mystery man stood about six foot three, skin as smooth as caramel. He had a head full of curly hair that was pulled back into a tight low ponytail. He had gorgeous hazel eyes, and when he smiled, Jonnae melted as the sight of the deepest dimples she had ever seen. She couldn't move, but the silence was broken when the man spoke.

"Hey Lil mama, what's your name?" He questioned.

After what seemed like a lifetime, Jonnae finally found her voice, "I'm Jonnae." She blushed, she never seen a man so fine. Yes Chink was fine, but this man was perfect.

"I'm Capo; don't mean to be so quick, but I gotta run, so let me get your number and I'll give you a call."

Jonnae dropped her head, "I have a boyfriend." Shakeisha nudged her.

Capo smiled, "Hey, I'll just give you my number and when you're ready, give me a call. Aight beautiful?"

Jonnae couldn't help but blush, "sure."

She pulled out her HTC Sensation. As Capo punched in his number, he laughed. "Soon as you call me, we're upgrading this tired ass phone."

Jonnae frowned, "Funny; when my boyfriend first approached me two years ago, he said the same thing. I happen to like my phone."

He laughed again, "Aye, don't worry about it. But I gotta run, be sure to use that number too." He flashed his million dollar smile again and Jonnae's panties instantly became wet.

'This man is fuckin gorgeous!' Jonnae thought to herself. She watched as Capo purchased a cigarillo and a strawberry kiwi Arizona.

Boy if you ever, left my, my side, it'd be like taking the sun from the sky, I'd probably die without you in my life, cuz I need you to, shine, shine your light, you're everything to me Jonnae quickly grabbed her phone as Monica's *Everything To Me* blared. She knew it was Chink.

As Capo was walking out the door, he turned and said, "Aight ma, I'll be expecting a phone call." She nodded.

"Hello" Jonnae answered.

"What's up ma, where are you?" Chink questioned.

"Heading back to Keisha's, why?" Jonnae wasn't feeling the fact that Chink was questioning her.

"Oh, I thought you were here. I'm sitting outside her house. I figured we'd grab lunch or something," Chink responded. He really wanted to make sure she wasn't getting any ideas to leave him. He didn't know how to deal with that.

"We're around the corner. We'll be there in a second." Jonnae figured she'd ask him about Lena.

"Aight bae, I'm here." With that said, they hung up. Jonnae turned to Shakeisha, "I'm gonna bring up that Lena chick to Chink."

"Girl, you gotta do what you gotta do. You know I'll back you. Besides, you know fine ass Capo wants you and damn does the name Capo fit him, cuz he sure does look like a fuckin BOSS!" They laughed.

As they turned onto Shakeisha block, they saw the block hoe, Tayla, talking to Chink. From the look on his face, you could tell he was ready to knock the fuck out of her. "Keisha, let me get this nigga outta here before I go nuts on this broad." Keisha understood and just nodded. Jonnae walked up to the driver's side of Chink's 2007 black Nissan Maxima.

"Let's go!" She demanded. "Keisha, I'll call you later."

Chink smiled, "Sorry, wifey calls." He jumped in the car as Jonnae turned up one of her favorite songs so it blared through the Bose speakers. *Bitch I be ridin through my old hood, but I'm in my new whip, same ol' attitude but I'm on that new shit.* Chink threw up the peace sign as Jonnae peeled off.

Shakeisha laughed, "That's a bad bitch!"

Tayla sucked her teeth, "Oh please! Ain't shit bad about that bitch. She thinks she's the shit cuz she got Chink; little does she know everyone's had him."

Shakeisha glared at her, "yeah, bitch, everyone but you. That's your problem, you always hate on the next bitch. And talk greasy about my girl again and I'm gonna smack the shit outta you!" Shakeisha walked away leaving Tayla there looking dumbfounded.

Chapter 6

As Jonnae drove, Chink kept glancing at her. *'She's so fuckin* beautiful' he thought. Jonnae felt his stare, "What?" she asked.

"I'm just thinking about how beautiful you are." He replied.

"Nigga don't try it, what the fuck was Tayla doing all in your face?"

Chink sucked his teeth, "Man, soon as I hung up with you, here she comes out her house dressed in damn near nothing tryna get a niggas attention. Ain't no one worried about that girl. I got who I want." Chink reached over and squeezed her leg.

"Who's Lena?" Jonnae questioned.

Chink scrounged his face up, "what are you talking about? Who the fuck wants a hoe like Lena?"

"Obviously you; especially since she's knocked up with your kid. So congrats on your baby. You'll make a great daddy," Jonnae spat with sarcasm.

"Hold the fuck up, let's rewind! Yes, I'll admit when we were broken up, yes I fucked Lena but that was damn near a year ago! I heard that bitch is like three months pregnant. As many niggas she done slept with, ain't no telling who knocked that up. I only see her when I'm passing through the hood." Chink exclaimed.

Before Chink knew it, Jonnae hauled off and smacked the shit outta Chink. She had tears streaming down her face. "Muthafucka, I don't care if we break up every fuckin day, that doesn't give you the right to fuck someone else. A hoe at that! Shit, I don't know who's worse; Tayla or Lena! Damn Chink; really? I have never slept with anyone else even if we were 'broken up'. That's fuckin bullshit! I can't believe you!"

Jonnae pulled the car over and jumped out. "Fuck the lunch date, and fuck you" Jonnae screamed. She started walking down the street. She was about fifteen minutes away from her house walking. Chink got out of the car and chased her.

"Bae wait, I'm sorry. I was fucked up and I'm sorry. Ma, please believe me, I'm nothing without you! You are my everything, my fuckin world, yo. I'll go crazy without you; please ma." It hurt Chink to see Jonnae in tears, especially because he was the cause of it.

Jonnae hated how much she loved Chink. She didn't understand why she loved him so much, despite all he's done to her.

"Chink, I wanna be alone."

Chink became aggravated, "Nah, every time we have a disagreement, you wanna be alone. For once, can we talk shit out? Damn Jonnae."

She wasn't in the mood for arguing with him anymore, "Whatever Chink!"

Chink could tell by her demeanor, that he was losing her. If he didn't change, he was gonna lose his one true love. Jonnae got back in the car and they proceeded on with their lunch date.

****

Jonnae and Chink finished up their school year strong. Jonnae finished with all A's and B's. Chink got good enough grades to get his high school diploma; and that was all he wanted. He really didn't see college in his future. Not yet anyway.

Jonnae wanted to go to college, but she didn't know how she would pay for it. He mother worked two jobs just to maintain the house and basic needs. She knew she had to figure out something.

As she sat on her bed scrolling through her newsfeed on Facebook, she thought about Capo. They had spoken a few times. He would usually text her during the day and call her at night. She reflected back on their first conversation almost a month ago.

Jonnae sat nervously on the phone while she waited for Capo to answer the phone.

"Yo" she heard him say.

"Hi, can I speak to Capo please" she spoke softly.

"Who's this" she heard him lower the music in the background.

"Jonnae" she hoped he remembered her because she waited two weeks before she called.

"Hey beautiful, I thought that was you. I started to think you forgot about me."

She smiled; she could never forget about that beautiful smile and those perfect dimples.

"No; I just have been busy with school and college searches."

He was impressed, "So you wanna go to college, huh? I like that."

She blushed, "yeah, I do."

He laughed, "Hey, how old are you ma?"

"I'll be eighteen on October seventh" she replied.

"Oh, you're still a baby. Let me be careful. You probably have a father or older brother lurking in the background" he laughed.

Jonnae chuckled, "actually, I don't know my punk ass daddy and my brother Boog is finishing off a three year bid. He should be out by this time next year, maybe earlier if he has good behavior."

"I take it you're close to your brother" Capo asked.

At that moment, Jonnae glanced over at the picture of her and Boog on her fourteenth birthday.

"Yeah, he's my heart. Only male figure I've had" Jonnae sighed and remembered she had to write Boog.

"Listen ma, I'm about to go get my hair braided up, so I'm gonna text you, is that cool" he asked.

Jonnae thought and figured it would give her the time to write Boog, "yeah, that's cool."

"Aight ma, I'll talk to you."

They said their goodbyes and hung up.

Jonnae laid across her bed as she listened to her iPod. She had Capo on her mind especially after she thought of their first conversation. She tried to limit the time she talked to him because she was still very much in love with Chink; or so she thought. At that moment, a song played on her iPod that forced her to think about her relationship and the ups and downs of it.

You and I were supposed to go our separate ways, no matter how much I fight, but still I stay, I can't believe my conscious got the best of me, it's telling me to let it go but I can't walk away, ya sista called me about a couple times today, she knew I had to get something off my mind right away, I gotta get a grip I think I'm losing it, I don't know why I'm so confused.

Silent tears rolled down Jonnae's face as she listened to the depth of the song and it felt like Olivia was telling her to walk away. Love wasn't supposed to hurt as much as it did. Right then and there, she decided that she gave Chink too much of her and was ready to take it all back. This was the end. No more crying, no more fighting over him, if he really loved and cared about her, she wouldn't have had to go through and do the shit she did for him. She watched her mother struggle and she didn't want to be that person.

Chapter 7

Jonnae realized she done too much lounging around for the day and decided to get started on doing something. She plugged her iPod into her iHome and blasted a song that was starting to grow on her. She didn't consider herself a gold digger but if you couldn't do shit for her, why even waste her time.

She turned the iHome up as loud as it went and sang along with Diamond's song "Lotta Money". For the next hour, Jonnae cleaned her room and sang her heart out. She knew this was the new beginning she deserved. Once she finished, she called Chink to set up a time and place to meet with him. She had written him a letter explaining why she was doing what she was doing. She knew she would be able to get the words out better in writing than in speaking. They agreed to meet up at the local burger spot, Five Guys around two o'clock. Jonnae finished straightening up her room and got dressed so she could start her journey to Five Guys.

Jonnae walked into the restaurant at one forty-five and she spotted Chink sitting in the booth near the window. She felt her palms beginning to sweat. She hoped that Chink would understand why she was doing what she was doing. She walked over and sat down directly across from him.

"Hi" she said barely above a whisper

"Hey ma, what's wrong" Chink knew something was wrong with his love.

"Nothing" she replied.

Chink knew she was lying, but he left it alone. They got up to order their food. They got their food and sat down and began eating. They made small talk and even shared a few laughs. Jonnae second guessed herself and asked herself if this was what she really wanted. The answer was no, it wasn't what she wanted, but it was what she needed. If she didn't do it now, she would forever deal with the drama that she currently was dealing with.

Before they knew it, forty five minutes passed. Jonnae sighed and pulled the letter out of her back pocket. She felt the tears building in the corner of her eyes. *Better get it done and over with now instead of dragging it out.*

"Chink" she whispered.

"Wassup ma," he replied.

"You know I love you with all my heart right?"

"Yeah, and you know I love you too. What's wrong?"

She sighed, "Words can't explain how much I love you, it's almost like I feel complete when I'm around you. I've been trying to figure out what it is that I possibly could have done that made you cause me so much hurt, but I can't seem to figure it out for the life of me. I feel like I have been the best girlfriend I could have possibly ever been. Yet it wasn't good enough for you."

"Jonnae what are you talking about? It seems like you're talking in circles."

The tears started rolling down her cheeks, "I can't do this anymore Erick. In the beginning everything was good. I was confident that I was your one and only. I knew I was the only one you wanted. I knew I was the woman you wanted to be with. Now I'm not sure about any of it. I don't know how many times you've cheated on me, yet I've accepted you back with open arms even when I knew letting you go was the smart thing to do. I knew I was making a stupid move but my love for you overpowered everything. That phone call from Lena was the icing on the cake. Granted you say it happened a while ago, but at the same time, it shouldn't have happened at all."

Jonnae's tears were flowing like a river. Chink's heart broke but he knew she was right. Jonnae was way better off without him. Yes, he loved her more than anything in the world, but he didn't know how to change and the last thing he wanted to do was constantly cause her more hurt than happiness. The night of his senior prom, he knew he was gonna lose her; he just didn't want to admit it.

"Jonnae, I'm so sorry for everything; I truly am. The last thing I ever wanted to do was cause you pain. I'll admit, I've made some fucked up decisions and choices and I wish I could take them all back. I'd do anything to see that beautiful smile that I used to see every day. Every time I see you shed a tear, my heart breaks, especially when I realize that I'm the cause of it. If what you want is time away from me, then I have no choice but to accept that and give you what you want. If that is what will make you happy then so be it." Chink's eyes began to water.

Jonnae leaned in and kissed Chink and as she pulled back, she slid the letter across the table. "Read this whenever you get the chance, and know my true feelings was poured into this letter. Take your time and then call me when you're ready to talk."

Jonnae got up and walked away and with each step she took, Chink's heart broke more and more. A tear threatened to fall from Chink's eyes. As he watched Jonnae disappear down the street, he thumbed the letter. In all honesty, he was afraid to open it because he didn't know what to expect. He sighed as he unfolded the letter. He scanned over Jonnae's perfect handwriting as he began to read.

By the time you read this letter, our relationship has probably ended. It's nothing that I wanted to do, but it is something that I had to do for myself. We've been together for almost three years and I have never ever loved anyone as much as I love you. Throughout these past three years, I've had some of the best times of my life. You brought the light into my life. You fit right into my life like the piece of a puzzle. You were the Quincy to my Monica, the Jody to my Yvette, you've held the key to my heart. From the first day I saw you, I knew you had to be mine, but I never knew you would cause me as much hurt as you did. The first year and a half of our relationship was perfect, romantic dates, movie nights, our conversations, everything. And then it all changed. You made me feel like I stopped being the girl you wanted. Yes you told me I was who you wanted, but you showed me different. What did I ever do for you to cheat on me in the first place? When I first asked you this question, you told me it was a stupid mistake and it would never happen again. I believed you and took you back, but yet again, I found myself fighting chicks who claimed to be sleeping with MY man. I found myself shedding tears at night wondering where I went wrong and why I couldn't be the only woman you wanted, yet my heart still remained in the palm of your hands. Remember the promise you made me? You told me, 'I promise to be the one who keeps the smile on your face and I promise to be the one who hurts the one who causes you to shed tears.' Can you hurt you? Chink all I ever wanted was for you to love me and only me. At first, I thought I had that, but I guess I was wrong. Remember when I went to Florida with my mother and I called you and I told you, I didn't want to talk, I just wanted you to listen to a song that described what my heart wanted to tell you, and I played, 'Soon As I Get Home' by Faith Evans. No words were needed because the song said enough. Remember prom night you sang to me? I felt like I was on top of the world, because that's what it felt like being around you. But lately it's like I can't even enjoy you because there's always drama. My heart is truly broken because I don't want anyone but YOU, but it's obvious you want everyone BUT ME! So I guess that's why I have to let it go right? If it's meant to be, God will lead us back together, but we're both young and it's obvious you're not ready to be as serious as I am, so why not let you free when it seems to be what you want. Never question it though, you are and always will be my first love and I will always love you with all my heart, but for me to allow you to constantly keep hurting me, makes me look stupid. Whenever you feel up to talking or expressing yourself, you have my number! I LOVE YOU ERICK MONTRELL JACKSON! Love always Jonnae.

When Chink finished reading the letter, he felt like the wind was knocked out of him. It took everything in him to not break down and cry right there in Five Guys. He sighed, stood and left the restaurant.

Chapter 8

As Jonnae walked home, she scrolled through the songs on her iPod. All the wrong songs were playing; they were her favorites, but not the ones she wanted to hear at that moment. One song stuck out that she just couldn't force herself to change it.

Feels so wrong, but I know it's right, should've been gone but I thought us was worth a fight, do you think of me, while doing you, the damage is done, you can't fix it this time, no more mister fix it, fix, fix, fix it up, you can't come back around, and try to clean it up, I gave you chance after chance and that was more than enough, said you'll do better next time, but there won't be a next time.

As she reached her house, her tears started falling and she didn't even bother to wipe them because she knew that she had to eventually cry her emotions out. As she listened to Tynisha Keli singing about there not being a Next Time; she ran through the house to get to her room. Her heart hurt, and it hurt badly. She didn't even feel this type of pain when Boog got locked up. Her heart was truly broken. She never imagined that she would be without Chink. She eventually cried herself to sleep.

Jonnae woke up three hours later to the ringing of her house phone. She reached over and grabbed the cordless off her dresser.

"Hello" she answered sleepily.

"You have a prepaid call from the Adult Correctional Facility from 'Boog' if you wish to accept this call, please press 0"

Jonnae perked up and pressed 0. She rubbed her eyes as the call was connected.

"Hey Boog" Jonnae smiled

"Hey baby girl, what's wrong with my sister?"

She sighed, "I'm alright Boog, hurt but alright."

"What's wrong Nae? You know damn well you can't hide shit from me" he chuckled.

"Chink and I broke up today. I've had enough of the hurt." Jonnae felt the tears building up in her eyes.

Boog sighed, "Damn Nae, I'm sorry to hear that. But what have I always told you?"

"If it was meant to be, it'll fall back together" they replied in unison.

Jonnae and Boog chatted for a little while longer. Jonnae could not wait until Boog got home. She missed having her brother around. They used to stay up late and tell each other jokes or they would wrestle with each other. Boog made sure that Jonnae would never have to worry about not being able to protect herself.

She found herself staring at the ceiling and less than twenty minutes later, sleep overcame her. Several hours later, she heard her house front door close. She glanced over at her digital clock and noticed it was after midnight. No one ever came through the door after midnight unless it was her. She got out of bed and slowly crept out the room. She heard two voices, one she recognized as her mom's and the other she didn't recognize. She slowly walked downstairs and followed the voices which led to the kitchen.

"Hey ma, you're just getting home" Jonnae questioned.

Her mother jumped, "oh hey baby, I didn't know you were up. This is my friend Gary. Gary, this is Jonnae, my daughter."

Jonnae didn't miss the lust in Gary's eyes and he instantly made her feel uncomfortable. She glanced back over at her mom, her mom smiled at Gary.

"Ma, are you okay?"

"Yeah, I'm fine baby. Go on back to bed."

Jonnae noticed the slurring in her mom's words which was unusual because her mom very rarely drank. She knew something was up especially because she brought a total stranger into the house. When she looked back at Gary, she noticed him lick his lips sexually. She decided in the morning that she would have a talk with her mom about Gary.

She turned on her heels and made her way back upstairs.

When Jonnae got to her room, she instantly closed and locked her door. She didn't like the way Gary was looking at her. She laid in the dark; she couldn't feel comfortable with Gary being there especially with the way he was looking at her. She tossed and turned for a little while. She grabbed her phone and noticed she had a missed call from Capo and a text message. She read the message before she returned the call.

hey ma, I was jus c'n wht yu were duin , feel free to call me weneva u get tha chance

She smiled and called his phone. She patiently waited for him to answer the phone. She heard him answer the phone and turn the music down.

"What's up beautiful?"

She blushed, she found herself always blushing when he called her beautiful, "nothing I just seen that you had called. What you up too" she asked.

"Nothing I'm on my way home right now. Ain't too much shit on these streets plus these young niggas are making the block hot."

She chuckled, "I hear you, that's why I don't do shit. If I ain't with Keisha, I'm home."

"You don't chill wit ya man" Capo questioned.

Jonnae sighed, "I don't have one anymore. I finally realized that I deserve so much better than being lied to and cheated on. Don't get me wrong, I love him but I deserve better."

Capo smiled at hearing that Jonnae no longer had a boyfriend but he wasn't gonna push up on her. He knew the healing process of ending a relationship that lasted years. His own heart was still healing, but he did a very good job at hiding it. "That sucks ma, but like you said, you deserve better. You deserve to be treated like royalty and nothing less."

Jonnae and Capo chatted until way after two am when Capo realized Jonnae fell asleep on the phone. "Good night beautiful. Sleep tight and sweet dreams." He knew she was sleep because he could hear the light snoring but he still said it.

Chapter 9

Jonnae woke up to the ringing of her cell phone. Without looking she answered the phone.

"Hello" she spoke with her eyes still closed.

"You finally got the point huh bitch" the caller stated.

"Who is this" she was now awake and not too happy.

"Ya worse fuckin nightmare! Stay away from Chink."

Jonnae sighed, she picked up on the voice as soon as they said Chink's name.

"Listen you thirsty ass bitch, hop the fuck off my pussy! If Chink really wants ya birdbrain ass, he would have been with you. Go get a fuckin life!"

The more she spoke to the girl; she realized her decision to leave Chink was a good one. As she sat there and listened to Tayla talk shit, she asked herself *'why am I even entertaining this bitch and her nonsense'.* She hung up right in Tayla's ear. She rubbed her eyes and looked at the clock. *'It's only ten am. What the fuck, I'm about sick of being woken up from bullshit.'* She rolled outta bed and went into the bathroom to handle her business. When she reached the sink, she instantly felt the tears in her eyes because she noticed Chink's hair brush and toothbrush on the sink. She missed him terribly but she knew what she did was for the good. She had to get Chink to get his things from her house or she would never be able to feel over him.

She made her way downstairs and towards the kitchen. She noticed a man sitting at the table in nothing but boxers and a t-shirt and that's when she remembered that Gary was in the house. She instantly ran upstairs and changed from her t-shirt into pajama pants and a wife beater. She made her way back to the kitchen. She noticed her mother at the stove. She walked over to the fridge to pull out the juice.

"Good morning ma. What you cooking?"

"Morning Nae and just making Gary a quick omelet."

Jonnae froze, "so just Gary is getting breakfast?" She was surprised because her mother never cooked breakfast for just one person, even when Chink spent the night; he got breakfast so she didn't understand this new one person breakfast thing.

"That's what I just said. Fend for yourself. You're damn near grown."

Jonnae's mouth hit the floor. Her mother never EVER acted the way she was acting now. "Ma, what the hell has gotten into you? The hell crawled up your ass and died?"

Her mother sucked her teeth, "first of all, swear again, and I'm gonna punch your teeth down your throat. Second of all, I'm grown, don't question me. I'm the mother around here. Don't forget it." All the while, her mother's back was facing her.

Gary snickered, "nigga I don't know why your ass is snickering. Ain't shit funny." Jonnae made her way quickly from the kitchen before her mother could react. She had to get out the house before she flipped the fuck out. Her mother never acted this way before, and she knew something was up, especially from her drunken night the night before and her actions this morning. Jonnae quickly took a shower and got dressed. It wasn't even noon, but she had to get out the house. She made her way towards Shakeisha house.

Fifteen minutes later, she turned onto Shakeisha street and was surprised to see a familiar car on the block. She continued down the street and as she did, her stomach started turning in knots. She said a silent prayer as she got closer. *'God please let my gut be lying to me. Just this once, I don't need any more hurt.'* She just knew she was going to see something she didn't want to see. She could feel it. She made her way up to Shakeisha door and turned the knob. Surprisingly it was unlocked.

"Hello" Jonnae called. She made her way towards Shakeisha room. She heard soft moans and her stomach knotted tighter. She poked her head into Shakeisha door since it was cracked, and what she seen, made vomit fly from her mouth before she could contain it. Her gag caused both Shakeisha and the man she was with jump and look at the door. Jonnae tried to hold in her tears as she back peddled out the room.

Chapter 10

Jonnae tried to run out the house without falling anywhere or knocking anything over.

"Jonnae wait"

"FUCK YOU SHAKEISHA! You ain't shit, I trusted you and you went and pulled that shit!?"

Shakeisha ran after Jonnae to stop her. She grabbed her arm as she reached the front door. "Jonnae listen to me for a minute will you? Damn!"

"Shakeisha what the fuck can you say that can justify that you were fucking my ex-boyfriend!? What the fuck, I mean we haven't even been broken up for a good twenty-four hours. You couldn't wait to sink your claws into what was mine? I fuckin trusted you with my life yet you go and do this? Go to fuckin hell!" Jonnae tried to turn around and walk out, but Shakeisha stopped her again.

"Shakeisha Nyelle Smith, you have two seconds to let go of me before I knock your lights out."

Shakeisha let go, but she still tried to get Jonnae to stay. "Jonnae please, let me explain."

Jonnae crossed her arms, "you have two minutes, so start fuckin talking."

She looked up the stairs, and noticed Chink standing there with his head hung low leaning on the railing. She instantly became disgusted and felt like spitting on him.

"Look Jonnae, I am so sorry. I never meant to hurt you."

Jonnae twisted her face, "You never meant to hurt me? Bitch you fucked my man and you're supposed to be my best friend. I came crying to YOU when he hurt me. I told you about him cheating on me with every other bitch and one of the bitches was you. You're fuckin grimy man. Shakeisha we've been friends since fuckin elementary school. You let a nigga come between us. Why didn't you just fuckin tell me you wanted him? With all the shit he put me through; I probably would have let his ass go. But to walk in on you fuckin him, talk about a fuckin low blow. I have two questions, and then I'm walking out of this door and out your life for good. How fuckin long and why?"

Shakeisha dropped her head. Jonnae shook her head and chuckled.

"This is fuckin sad!! The two people I trusted betrayed me In the worst way ever. And YOU!" she pointed to Chink "after I just poured my fuckin heart out to you, obviously I don't mean shit to you. You ungrateful piece of shit. Why? Of all the chicks in the muthafuckin state, you choose my best friend? How fuckin low can you get?"

She turned back to Shakeisha, "Answer my question Keisha! How fuckin long and why?"

Shakeisha sighed, "About six months and I honestly don't know why. Maybe it's because you always talked about him cheating on you, maybe now you'll see he ain't shit!"

Jonnae crinkled her brows, "so you did this to prove a point? Bitch, ONE time will prove a point, but for six months is a fuckin back stabbing move. As my best friend, you're supposed to listen to me vent dumbass!! Is this why you constantly told me Chink wasn't right for me? Because you wanted him for yourself?" she chuckled "I can't believe I was blind to this. Man y'all two conniving bastards are made for each other. And here I am thinking I may have been too hard on you and thinking about giving us a try again, HA, glad I found this out. Dirty muthafuckas." With that, Jonnae walked out the door and out both Shakeisha and Chink's lives. She was tempted to pull a Jazmine Sullivan and bust the windows out Chink's car but she wasn't stooping down to a childish level. Instead she held her head high and walked. She had no destination in mind, she just walked.

A half hour later, Jonnae realized she had walked the same block maybe three times. She was hurt and she couldn't even lie about it. Right now all she wanted was someone to talk too. As she passed Saki's pizza for the third time, she decided to actually go inside and grab a slice and try to clear her head. She couldn't believe the betrayal. She wasn't surprised that Chink was cheating, but more so who he was cheating with! Shakeisha though? Her best friend since elementary school. It was a hard pill to swallow.

Jonnae got her pizza and sat down. Soon as she slid into the booth, she lost her appetite. She allowed a lone tear to slide down her cheek. She took a deep breath and wiped the tear but kept her eyes closed.

"Now why is my pretty lady shedding tears?"

Her ears perked up at the sound of the voice. She smiled when she noticed Capo sitting across from her.

"Oh my gosh, I'm embarrassed. Guess I was so into my own thoughts, I didn't even notice you. Sorry about that." she quickly wiped her eyes.

"Why is such a beautiful lady crying tears of sadness?"

Jonnae sighed, "It's only going on what, one thirty, and my day has already been shot to shit." Jonnae scoffed, "I don't even know who to trust anymore." She dropped her head and tried to fight the tears. She was absolutely tired of shedding tears over someone who didn't deserve her.

Capo reached over and lifted her chin so she would look into his eyes, "listen mami, I don't know who hurt you or did whatever to you, but I promise you, you can always, and I mean ALWAYS trust me. I put my life on that."

Jonnae smiled. She felt comfortable around Capo, but after the ordeal with Chink, she put a lock around her heart.

"Thanks, I really appreciate it. I'll be honest, I feel lonely as fuck. What do you do when the two people you trusted with your life, betray you in the worse way possible?"

Capo sat back, "to be honest, I'd probably try to handle it the street way first, which is tryna fuck them up, but the right way, is to ask yourself, 'do you need that in your life' and if your answer is no, then you take your pride and keep it moving, no matter the amount of pain."

Jonnae thought about what Capo just said and realized he was right. It was both Keisha and Chink's loss. She did nothing wrong but be the best girlfriend and best friend she knew how to be. Capo and Jonnae chatted for a little and she had to truly admit, she loved the time she spent with Capo. Before they both knew it, three hours and an entire large pizza went by.

Chapter 11

The constant ringing of Capo's phone finally became annoying and he decided to answer it.

"Pea, as much as you just blew up my phone, this shit better be life or death."

"It is nigga, you know I would never blow ya shit up like that if it wasn't something major."

Capo didn't like the sound of Peanut's voice.

"Talk to me Pea"

Peanut sighed, "Nigga Janiylah is in the hospital"

Just to make sure he heard him right, Capo asked him to repeat what he said.

"You heard me right, ya little sister, Janiylah is in the hospital"

The wind felt like was knocked right out of Capo's chest.

"What the fuck you mean my sister is in the hospital. Peanut, what the hell is going on" Capo yelled, causing him to gain the attention from the surrounding patrons.

"Man, that nigga Bone rode up on me asking where you were because ya sister was in the hospital. Word is she was raped and thrown out on the street like she wasn't shit. This shits fuckin with me man, I see Janiylah like a little sister too"

Capo stood and waved for Jonnae to follow him. He dropped forty dollars on the table and walked out. Although she walked there, he wasn't about to allow her to walk home. Especially with the news he just received.

Capo listened as Peanut told him all the details he knew. Both he and Jonnae jumped into his car and he took off like a bat out of hell. He was so into his conversation with Peanut about Janiylah, he forgot to even drop Jonnae off at home. Before they knew it, they were pulling up in front of Providence Children's Hospital.

Capo ran into the emergency room and straight up to the counter. This all felt too familiar to him. "I'm looking for Janiylah Turner"

"Are you her parent" the receptionist asked.

"I'm her older brother." Capo replied.

"We need her parents."

He lost it, "Our mother is dead and unless you're gonna give every nigga in the world a DNA test, I suggest you tell me where my sister is."

Jonnae rubbed his back to try and soothe him.

The receptionist looked taken aback, "I'm sorry sir. She's in room 20."

Capo took off with Jonnae hot on his heels. They walked into the room and Capo's knees buckled. Jonnae held onto him so he wouldn't fall. His sister's face was bandaged and he could see the bruise around her eyes. His eyes began to water. Janiylah must've sensed him because she looked right in his direction.

"Hey Ja'kahri"

"Niylah what the fuck happened? Who did this?"

Janiylah looked away, "Ja'kahri I'm sorry"

"Fuck all the sorry shit Janiylah, who the fuck did this"

"BK"

Jonnae's eyes became wide. She had to ask, "Do you know his real name"

Capo looked at her like she was crazy. Janiylah looked at her, "if I'm not mistaken its Keith"

Jonnae knew exactly who she was talking about. Jonnae shook her head as she thought of her own secret that no one knew about. She hated BK with a passion and knew one day he would get his. If Capo handled him, he'd be doing both Janiylah and Jonnae a favor.

Chapter 12

Jonnae stepped out of the room as Janiylah and Capo continued their conversation. Hearing BK's name brought back serious memories and forced her to travel down memory lane.

Jonnae was fourteen years old and was walking home from Shakeisha house. She was about a block from her house when BK, a small time hustler approached her. She rejected him and continued on her way.

BK was adamant and continued following her. When Jonnae tried to run, he grabbed her, placing his hand over mouth. He threw her in the back of a car that seemed to appear out of nowhere. Jonnae fought and fought to get BK off of her but his one hundred eighty pound frame outweighed her one twenty any day.

As Jonnae cried and fought for her prized possession, BK and his boy who drove the car took turns raping her. After torturing her for over an hour, they finally let her go. As she staggered home, she felt absolutely disgusted. She knew people were looking at her. She eventually started running as fast as her aching legs would take her. Ten minutes later, although it felt like ten hours, she finally made it home. She ran straight to the shower and scrubbed her body until she was red and raw. Even after all of that, she still felt nasty. It wasn't her fault, and she knew it wasn't her fault yet she blamed herself thinking she didn't fight hard enough, or long enough.

She never told anyone what happened to her. Not even Chink. She let him believe he was the one who took her virginity. The day after it happened, Jonnae went to a clinic, which dealt with situations like this and checked for any STDs as well as took a Plan B pill to ensure no pregnancy.

To hear that BK struck again tore Jonnae apart. She didn't realize she was crying until she felt the tear hit her chest. She quickly wiped it away as she heard footsteps approaching her. She turned around and seen Capo looking like he had the weight of the world on his shoulders.

Jonnae welcomed him with open arms because she knew he needed someone, especially at this point in time. Capo fell into Jonnae's arms and broke down. He had never cried in front of anyone. Not even his boys, yet here he was in the middle of the hospital breaking down in the arms of someone he barely knew.

Jonnae soothed him the best she could. She had no idea what to say so she didn't say anything. She just hugged him and allowed him to cry. Five minutes later, he got himself together and they both left the hospital.

"I'm sorry about that back there," Capo spoke without looking at her.

"No need for apologies. Everyone has to break down once in a while. I know mine is coming soon."

Capo looked at her, waiting to see if she would elaborate. They continued driving in silence.

"Do you mind if I stop by my house before I bring you home" Capo asked.

"Right now, I'd rather be anywhere BUT home. Its times like this I wish Boog were home."

'This girl has a story behind her. I can tell just by looking in her eyes. She needs someone to just listen to her clear her head.' Capo continued driving. He reached over and grabbed her hand.

"I meant what I said back at Saki's. You can always trust me. Never question it."

Chapter 13

Jonnae realized she wasn't in her neighborhood when Capo pulled up to a gated community full of flawless condominiums. Her mouth dropped and Capo chuckled as he drove into his driveway. Jonnae dreamed of living in one of these. That's all it was; a dream.

"If you like the outside, then you will love the inside." Capo grabbed Jonnae's hand and he reached for his keys and unlocked the door to his domain.

Jonnae stepped into the house and the very first thing she noticed was the shiny, polished floor. They were so shiny; she could see her reflection. She knew she wasn't in the projects that she lived in. She looked and admired the wrap around staircase that led to the second floor of the home. Her feet felt planted to the floor as she admired the home and noticed the crystal chandelier hanging from the ceiling. As she looked to her right, she noticed the black and red living room. The walls were painted red and were covered with photos. There was one portrait that stuck out to Jonnae. It sat over the mantel. She slowly walked towards it to study the people in the picture. It was a woman surrounded by three people. One, she instantly recognized as Capo, the younger lady, she recognized as his sister; but she didn't know who the other two were.

Capo noticed Jonnae staring at the picture. He walked up behind her. "That's my mom Jennisse. The other one is Jarell, you haven't met him and that's Janiylah." Jonnae could hear the sorrow in his voice. "Everything seemed to perfect then. Nothing could erase those smiles off of our faces. Shit changed last year."

Jonnae's interest was piqued, "what happened?"

Capo's eyes never left the picture as he spoke, "her last words still ring in my head. 'Get out the game, son. You walk away from it before it takes you.' That's the first thing I think about every morning when I wake up."

Jonnae took a step towards Capo as she watched his eyes glisten. "Where is she now?" She didn't want to seem nosey, but she wanted to know why he starred at the picture as hard as he did.

Capo hadn't spoken to anyone about the situation with his mom. It brought back too many painful memories. With Jonnae, he felt comfortable enough for him to lift burden off his shoulder. "The muthafucka that did that shit is lucky the streets caught up to him before I did. He beat and raped my mother."

Jonnae's heart crushed for Capo because she could see the genuine love and affection he had for his mother. To have to have gone through this situation again with his sister had to be eating him apart. Capo's mind traveled back down memory lane as he thought about the night that he pulled up to his mother's house.

Capo was wrapping up his business on the streets. He was

actually closing shop early because he had a nagging feeling that something was wrong. If it was one thing his mother taught him, it was always follow your gut instinct. He dapped up his boys and jumped in his car heading home. As he got closer and closer, his nagging feeling became stronger and stronger. Pulling up on his mom's street, he noticed the ambulance and police cars surrounding his mother's house. He stopped right in the middle of the street and jumped out the car and ran full speed to the front door.

The police stopped him at the caution tape, "you can't go in there sir"

"That's my mother's house so if someone in this house is hurt, it's one of my family members!" he screamed.

Just then, a stretcher came out the door with an oxygen mask over the patients face. Capo ran over to the stretcher and that's when his world came crashing down, his mother was laying on the stretcher with a battered face. He softly touched his mother's face. She fluttered her eyes open, "son" she whispered.

"Shh ma, please don't talk. Save your energy."

They loaded the stretcher into the ambulance and headed to the nearest hospital, Providence Memorial.

Capo jumped back into his car and followed the ambulance while calling his brother to fill him in on what happened. Jarell agreed to bring Janiylah with him up to the hospital. Capo rushed into the hospital desk. "I need the room of the patient that was just brought in here. Jennisse Turner."

"Sir, right now the doctors are in with her, but I will let them know that you are here. Can I have your name?"

"Ja'kahri Turner" Capo replied.

The receptionist nodded and Capo took a seat and began playing the waiting game. Ten minutes later, Janiylah and Jarell came flying into the waiting room.

"Kahri, what's going on?" Janiylah was in tears. Capo pulled her into a tight embrace and allowed her to cry on his shoulder.

The receptionist interrupted, "Mr. Turner, you can go in now. She's in the fourth room on your left."

Janiylah, Capo and Jarell raced to the room. Seeing their mother in such a condition broke all of their hearts. She had IV's coming out of her arm and hand as well as a breathing tube in her nose. Capo approached her bedside first. Jarell held onto Janiylah so she wouldn't fall.

"Mama....mama can you hear me?" Capo was getting choked up but he knew with him being the oldest, he had to be strong.

Her eyes fluttered, "Hey son. Where's your brother and sister."

Capo waved his brother and sister to the bedside. Something in him was telling him this wasn't going to end as he planned.

"I want all you guys to know, I love you to death. Nothing

or no one can ever change that. You came from me; you all are a replica of me in some way. Ja'kahri, you have my brains book and street smart. You can pass any test with flying colors but you also can do the same thing in the streets. You can smell a rat from a mile away. It comes with being in the streets, but son, Get out the game. You walk away from it before it takes you. Jarell, you have my hustle. Anything you want, you bust your ass to get it even if it means spending your last on it. Janiylah, my beautiful Janiylah. You are me all over again growing up. I love the woman you are becoming. Please, continue it and never let anyone stop you."

Janiylah spoke up, "Ma stop, you're sounding like this is the last time we are gonna see you."

Before Jennisse could respond, she began coughing uncontrollably. Her heart monitor started beeping loudly alerting the doctors and nurses. He listened to the machine flat line. Capo couldn't believe that would be the last time he saw his beautiful mother alive.

Chapter 14

Before Capo realized it, he felt a tear rolling down his cheek. This was the second time in one day that he cried in front of Jonnae and he wasn't even embarrassed to say he did so. Something about her, made him feel beyond comfortable. He understood that she just got out of a relationship, but he was willing to wait for her, no matter how long it took. Capo wiped his face and finished giving Jonnae the tour of his home. With every room they went into, she fell more and more in love with it.

I can see myself living here' "most definitely" she said out loud without realizing it. Jonnae and Capo made their way back to the kitchen. Jonnae sat on the bar stool while Capo stood on the other side of the counter.

"Tell me about you Ms. Jonnae. What are your goals and dreams? Where do you see yourself ten years from now?"

She thought for a second. "Well for starters, I don't see myself living in Rhode Island for much longer. I would love to see what the dirty south is all about." They shared a laugh. "I wanna finish high school, and even go to college. I see my mom bust her ass to take care of me, and I don't wanna struggle. I mean I know nothing is easy, but I don't wanna have to work two jobs just to maintain, ya know? Hopefully once Boog gets out of jail, I can convince him of a change of scenery." She paused as she thought of her brother.

"Your brother really means everything to you, huh?"

She smiled, "Yeah he does. He's the only male figure I've had in my life. When my mom worked late to provide, it was Boog who tucked me in at night, who sat with me when I was afraid to go to sleep, who assured me that no matter what, I would always have him. When he got locked up, I felt like a part of me went with him. I've never had a closer bond with anyone. Not even..." She stopped, she didn't even want to speak Shakeisha name after what happened earlier in the day.

Capo caught her pause, "Not even what?"

She shook her head, she wasn't sure she wanted to relive the scene. "Nothing; just forget it."

Capo thought back to earlier that day. "Jonnae are you gonna tell me what happened earlier that had you crying in the damn pizza parlor."

She sighed, "Betrayal at its finest."

"Keep going; you've seen me cry twice today so spill. If we're gonna be friends, mine as well start off with telling each other what is bothering us."

She began from the beginning. Starting with Tayla at prom night, the call from Lena, the breakup the day before, up until walking in on Chink and Shakeisha fucking, she told him everything. Capo was at a loss for words. He was stuck on the fact that her best friend would even cross that line. Jonnae was such a good girl, why Chink would fuck that up is beyond him. They chatted way into the late night. They learned so much about each other and became more interested in each other before the night was out. They agreed to keep it strictly a friendship, which gave Jonnae the proper healing time she needed.

Over the next few months, Jonnae's life was kind of up and down. Her upside was Capo. They'd become best friends since that day they spent together at Saki's. If they weren't together, they talked every day. They hadn't even had sex but it had been on both their minds. Both Shakeisha and Chink had tried to reach out to Jonnae but she wasn't having it.

Jonnae's downside was her home life. Gary damn near moved in, which meant Jonnae was only home to sleep and even then; she made sure her door was locked with a chair under the knob. Her mom picked up an alcohol and sadly, a drug problem as well. Jonnae spent as much time away from home as possible, whether she was in the library or hanging out with Capo. Shakeisha even tried to reach out to Jonnae at school, but Jonnae walked by her like she didn't exist. In her eyes, she didn't. Jonnae and another girl that lived in her neighborhood, Michelle, started kicking it. She didn't allow her to get as close as she allowed Shakeisha, but she kept her around as the female friend she needed. It hurt her that she couldn't trust Shakeisha, but Shakeisha brought that upon herself.

Chapter 15

Jonnae's birthday was rapidly approaching and she had absolutely no plans. Well no major plans. What she been planning for years, was shot to shit when the two people she planned on celebrating with betrayed her. Since Capo's birthday was two days before her, she figured she would just celebrate with him. Nothing big; just him and her maybe dinner or something. She would run the idea by him. His birthday was on a Thursday and hers was that Saturday.

She quickly shot Capo a text

Nae: Did yu have sttn planned fah our bdaysz?

She waited for his response as she watched her teacher's mouth move but didn't listen to anything that came out of it.

Capo: Not the time for this convo, pay attn in class dammit

She had to catch herself from laughing out loud. That was one thing she admired about Capo, he made sure her education was her number one priority.

The remainder of the day flew by. She walked outside with Michelle as she always did. She spotted Tayla standing on the stairs of the school talking to her group of floozies that hung around her.

"Bitch is still mad that Chink doesn't want that ass no more'"
Tayla snickered.

Jonnae ran her tongue across her teeth and flared her
nostrils.

"Jonnae, don't pay the broad no mind. You know the real
reason you and Chink ain't together and it damn sure ain't
got nothing to do with her," Michelle stated.

Jonnae and Michelle continued their way down the stairs.

"Look, the bitch is so hurt; she can't stand to look at me."
Tayla's group of friends laughed.

Jonnae stopped and turned around. "Tayla, really? You
wish the reason me and Chink aren't together is because of
your raggedy ass! If he EVER left me for you, it would be
such a major downgrade because bitch even on your best
day, you're not on my level. If you really are with Chink, like
you claim to be, then ask him why we ain't together. Your
name won't even come up."

With that, Jonnae turned and walked away. Tayla's jaw was
on the floor. Jonnae reached the bottom of the stairs when
she heard someone yell, "Watch your back, Jonnae!"

She turned around and caught Tayla before she could sneak
one. Tayla was a sneaky bitch, especially trying to catch her
with her back turned. She quickly dropped Tayla and
proceeded to take all her anger out on her. All the years of
crying over Chink, all the drama she went through with

Shakeisha, her mom's drug and alcohol problem, every frustration that she felt, Tayla was feeling.

Next thing she knew, she felt a pair of arms wrapping around her. That's when she realized that she had blacked out. "Come on ma, really? You are so much better than this." She recognized the voice as Capo's and for a reason unknown, she broke down crying. "Shhh ma, it's okay." Capo guided Jonnae to the car with Michelle in tow.

Michelle made sure Jonnae was okay before she proceeded to her car and took off.

"Bae, what happened back there? You pounced on ol' girl like she was nothing."

Jonnae scoffed, "In my eyes, she is nothing. That bitch ain't shit but trouble. She swears Chink wants her and shit but everyone and their mama knows, God himself don't want that bitch."

Capo busted out laughing, "Damn shawty, that's cold."

"Fuck it, it's true. That ain't the first time she done got her ass beat, but obviously she don't care because she keeps fuckin starting with me. She won't be happy until I fuckin break her face."

"I don't know if you saw her face, but that shit looked pretty broken to me." They shared a laugh. Jonnae couldn't lie, she enjoyed being around Capo and she was starting to catch feelings. It had been almost six months since her and Chink broke up. It felt good to be single, but she missed being taken sometimes.

Because Capo had something to do, he dropped Jonnae off at home; the last place she ever wanted to be. She walked in the door and Gary was sitting on the couch.

"Where is my mother?"

Gary had the lustful look in his eyes, "She ran to the store for me."

Jonnae rolled her eyes as she headed to the kitchen to grab ice for her hand. It was throbbing and she could see it beginning to swell.

Gary watched her with close eyes. Sadly, he lost all interest in Jonnae's mother, Rita, when he first laid eyes on her daughter. *One day, I'll have her, even if I have to take it* he sinfully thought. Jonnae noticed his stare and ran to her room. She locked her door and started on her homework. She figured she'd be done in an hour and she can head out somewhere. It was a Friday, bad enough she had homework but the sooner she left, the better.

As she was finishing up her history homework, she heard her doorknob rattle. She knew who it was, because he was the only one home.

"Wrong room" Jonnae yelled.

He continued to rattle the doorknob.

"What Gary" she shouted through the door.

"Open the door Jonnae."

"For what? My mother ain't here and there's nothing in here for you."

Before she knew it, he rammed his entire body into the door, busting it open. Jonnae's body instantly tensed up.

"Next time I tell you to open the door, you open the fuckin door."

Although she tried her best to hide it, Jonnae was completely petrified. She never missed the lust filled looks that Gary sent her way.

"Wha -- What do you want Gary" she stuttered. She tried not to allow the shakiness in her voice appear, but it did and Gary picked up on it. Gary noticed that she had changed. She no longer had on the outfit she wore to school, but now had an oversized hoodie on with short shorts. He groped his dick through his pants.

"Gary, can you please leave and shut the door. Well whatever is left."

Instead of walking out of her room, he walked in and closed the door behind him. She now regretted not putting her blade back under her pillow. If she tried to reach for it in her desk drawer, Gary would be on her like white on rice.

"Gary, I'm gonna ask you one more time..."

Before she could finish her sentence, he lunged at her. He caught her off guard and had all his body weight on her. Tears instantly sprang to her eyes as he placed one hand firmly around her throat and the other over her mouth. She fought hard to keep her emotions in check. She didn't want to show weakness by crying.

Gary roughly tried to pull down Jonnae's shorts as she tried to fight him. His two hundred twenty pound frame outweighed her one forty five. Jonnae could no longer fight the tears as she thought about how this would be the second time she would be raped and had no one to help her. Her body grew tired of fighting and for an hour straight, she laid there and allowed Gary to have his way with her.

Chapter 16

The night of the rape, Jonnae cried to herself. Once again, she felt completely disgusted. She couldn't look at herself in the mirror. She heard her phone constantly ringing, but she didn't want to move. After ringing for a half hour straight, she finally reached for her phone.

She saw Capo's picture displaying on her screen as he called her for the fifteenth time. She answered but said nothing.

When the phone connected, Capo heard sniffling.

"Jonnae?"

He heard soft cries.

"Ma, what's wrong?" His heart began racing.

"It happened again" she whispered.

Capo pressed the phone tightly against his ear, "Mami, I need you to speak louder. What happened?"

"It happened again Capo."

His heart stopped, "What happened again?"

"He raped me." With her just saying those words, she burst into tears.

He lost it, "WHO DID WHAT!?"

"Gary raped me" she was still whispering incase Gary was somewhere close.

Capo whipped his BMW around in the middle of an intersection, barely missing a passing car. He raced to Jonnae's house, which luckily was only around the corner.

He just listened to her cry as he sped to her house. "Hold on baby girl, I'm coming for you."

Five minutes later, he illegally parked his car in front of Jonnae's apartment building. He flew up the stairs to the second floor and pounded on the front door like he was the police. "Jonnae, ma it's me, open the door please."

She was afraid to move. She felt straight up disgusting in every sense of the word. She was just getting over the first rape but now here she was, raped in the comfort of her own home.

"Ma, please open the door."

Jonnae dragged herself out of her bed and to the front door. She wiped her swollen red face. As soon as she opened the door, she fell into Capo's arms and cried her heart out. Hearing the cries, Gary came out of her mother's bedroom and walked into the living room. Jonnae hugged Capo tighter knowing Gary was in the room.

The way that Capo glared at Gary, if looks could kill, Gary would have dropped dead right where he stood.

"Muthafucka, I promise you, I will see you" Capo seethed through clenched teeth. He scooped Jonnae up like she was his bride, and carried her to the car. Jonnae cried silently the entire ride. Capo drove her straight to his home. She had a zombie like look on her face. Capo stripped her out of her clothes and placed her in the warm bath water. He felt Jonnae relax in the water and before he knew it, she was crying.

"Shh, bae, it's gonna be okay. I promise you, I'm gonna take care of you."

"I feel damaged. No one will ever want me. I'm broken; no one wants a girl who has been raped not once but twice. I will never be loved. Chink didn't love me, Shakeisha didn't love me, my mother doesn't love me, and my piece of shit father doesn't love me. Only person that loves me is being held like a caged animal. I'm all alone out here."

Capo's heart broke listening to Jonnae cry. He also picked up on her saying she was raped twice, but figured he would question it later. A tear fell from his eye, he kissed Jonnae's forehead. "I love you Jonnae; flaws and all. I wish I could've protected you from the things you've gone through. I may not have been there before, but I'm here now and I vow to protect you as long as you allow me too. It'll be me and you against the world baby girl. Give it all to me, ma. Hand your problems over to me and let me take care of them."

Jonnae smiled through her tears. She looked at Capo deep

in his eyes. She knew his words were genuinely spoken.

After allowing Capo to clean her cuts and scrapes from her attack, she washed herself up. Her body ached and when she reached between her legs, she couldn't stop the tears from falling. Although Capo assured her that he wasn't fazed by her flaws, she still felt dirty.

Ten minutes later, she climbed out the shower and wrapped herself in an extra-large towel. She walked into Capo's bedroom as she adored the three inch thick plush carpet. Capo was sitting back on his bed leaning on headboard. Jonnae hadn't even sat on it but she loved the king size sleigh bed.

She stood in the middle of his room, just admiring the man she could see herself loving; if she already didn't.

He chuckled, "it's crazy, cable cost so much, and they still don't have shit on."

Jonnae laughed and shook her head because she knew it was true. She glanced down at the bed and saw a pair of Capo's basketball shorts and his t-shirt.

"I hope you don't mind. I don't have a closet full of woman's clothes."

She smiled, "no it's cool, but I wouldn't mind underclothes."

"Gimme your bra and panties size."

Jonnae looked at him sideways. He laughed.

"Chill shawty, there's a Burlington Coat Factory down the street that should be open, I'll run down there and grab you something quick, just to get through the night, and I'll bring you home tomorrow to get clothes.

The expression on her faced changed to one as if she had seen a ghost.

"You don't have to stay there if you don't want too, feel free to stay here" Capo stated.

"Size six panties and thirty six D bra" she replied.

He whistled, "Damn. I'll be back."

He hopped up, slipped on his Jordan flip flops, grabbed his wallet and keys and was out the door.

Chapter 17

Waiting for Capo to return, she flipped through the channels and stopped when she came across The First 48. As she was engrossed in the show, she heard vibrating. She looked around for her phone but found it sitting on the nightstand, not ringing. She then glanced at the dresser and noticed Capo's iPhone. She walked over and glanced at the screen. *Who the hell is Vanessa* she thought. She was tempted to answer but quickly dismissed the thought. Capo wasn't her man, not yet anyway.

She returned to the bed and waiting for Capo to come back. She never even heard him come in until he tossed the bag at her.

"Nigga, make noise."

He laughed, "Stop being such a punk."

She punched him in the arm and laughed. She got up and went to the bathroom to get dressed. While she was in the bathroom, she looked at herself in the mirror. At that moment, she made a vow to never allow another man to take advantage of her.

A few minutes later, she came out the bathroom and laid her head on Capo's lap. He never changed the channel, so they both watched The First 48.

"While you were gone, your phone was ringing" she stated.

"Did you answer it?"

She shook her head no.

"Why not?"

"It's not my phone to answer. But I did look at the screen. It said Vanessa."

Capo chuckled, "so you'll look at the screen, but you won't answer it. You walked that far, you should've just answered it."

She punched him playfully, "shut up. I didn't want to overstep my boundaries."

He cupped her chin and tilted her head up towards his, "I have nothing to hide from you, so if my phone rings and I'm not around, answer it."

Jonnae was taken aback. She was with Chink for almost three years and she was lucky if the phone left his hand, never mind telling her to answer it. She nodded and they continued watching the show.

Before she knew it, she was knocked out. Capo watched her sleep as he stroked her cheek. He then moved her over so she was laying on the bed. *She looks so peaceful. Why would anyone want to fuck up a relationship with her? Fuck it, his loss is my gain. I just hope and pray she won't do me dirty like Vanessa's grimy ass did.* As Capo watched Jonnae sleep, he thought about his two year relationship with Vanessa.

Capo met Vanessa when he was eighteen. He had always seen her around the hood and had a crush on her. He was never the type to push up on a female though so he sat back and hoped that she would recognize him.

One night, he was out at the club chilling with his boys Peanut and Tech. He had to pay the bouncer extra to get Tech and Peanut in because they were both underage. They sat back in the VIP section popping bottles all night. Capo wasn't a big drinker but he would sip here and there. He always liked being on point. As he was watching Peanut and Tech pop bottles and get drunk, he noticed Vanessa walking through the VIP rope. She looked amazing in her thigh high black Bebe dress. It made her apple bottom ass look even bigger. Capo's dick got hard just looking at her. She noticed him and made her way over. She sat on his lap and whispered in his ear, "you look fly as shit, but I'd like to see what you look like with nothing on." Straight to the point, like Capo liked them.

With Vanessa, he wanted to take it slow. Yeah, that night, he fucked the shit outta her, but she wasn't like the chicks he normally fucked. With others, he would fuck them and leave them high and dry, but with Vanessa, he wifed her up. Peanut, Tech and their boy Kali all said the relationship between the two wouldn't work. They tried to warn Capo about Vanessa, but he never listened so they allowed him to learn on his own.

The relationship between Capo and Vanessa was going

perfectly, up until they hit their two year mark. Vanessa had been pressing Capo about wanting kids, but with his lifestyle, he knew bringing a child into the world wasn't a smart idea. He made sure he never busted in Vanessa, always pulling out. He knew Vanessa wanted a baby, especially by him. It would secure her a stable life.

One day, Capo was home relaxing. He liked to take one day off out of the week to chill out and step away from the street life. Vanessa was in the shower and her phone was on nightstand charging. Capo tried to ignore the vibration but it was becoming annoying. He glanced at the screen, 'who the fuck is Tony' he thought. He placed the phone back on the nightstand and focused on the television again. Two minutes later, her phone vibrated alerting that there was a text message. Seeing it was from this Tony character, he opened the message.

Tony: Damn Ness, r u gunna keep ignorin me? Shit now, ya carryn my seed yet u ain't tryna let me know wat da fuck is goin on, iont care tht ya wit dis nigga kus u wuznt worried abt it b4, hit me back Ness, & im not askin either

Capo's heart fell to his stomach. He wanted to cry so badly but his pride wouldn't allow him too. He marched into the bathroom and slammed the glass door back into the wall so hard, it completely shattered! He grabbed Vanessa off her feet by her throat before she could even say anything.

"You're pregnant Vanessa" Capo's voice roared

Vanessa struggled to breathe. She clawed at his hand.

"Get your shit and get the fuck outta my house." He dropped her onto the shower floor. She coughed as she gasped for air.

Capo entered his bedroom, sat on the bed and threw his head into his hands. He was hurting, his heart was broken but he refused to shed tears.

Vanessa crept into the room; her face stained with tears

"Ja'kahri, talk to me."

"Fuck you want me to say Vanessa? You need to be the one talking."

She dropped her head, "I'm sorry, Kahri. I really am."

"Sorry for what? Being pregnant by another nigga or getting caught? And who the fuck is Tony?"

"BOTH! I never meant..."

Capo cut her off, "don't even say you never meant to hurt me! You don't give a fuck about my feelings. If you did, you wouldn't be knocked up by another nigga!"

She screwed up her face, "All I ever did was love you! You always too busy running the streets to see that. I get lonely, Ja'kahri, fuck was I supposed to do, wait forever!?"

Once the words came out, she realized how dumb she sounded.

"Bitch, YES you're supposed to wait! I'm your man, you

dummy. Bad enough you cheated, but you fucked the nigga raw and got fuckin pregnant. Man, get your shit and get the fuck outta my house shawty. I don't have time for this dumb shit. By the time I get back, have your shit gone and leave my key under the rug."

With that he turned and walked out the door. His heart shattered when she asked him if she was supposed to wait, "DUH bitch" he thought out loud. Capo jumped in his Escalade, turned up the radio to Biggie's "Get Money" and peeled out. He fired up a blunt and just drove. He had no set destination he just kept driving.

After driving for twenty minutes, he ended up at the beach. Ever since he was little, the water always helped him clear his head. He refused to call Peanut or Tech because he didn't want to hear "I told you so". At that moment, he made a vow that he would never be so vulnerable and love so hard again.

Chapter 18

Here he was, a year and a half later, finding himself falling for Jonnae. He didn't think that she wasn't anything like Vanessa; she was a good girl who wanted out of the hood. She was seventeen and already knew what she wanted to be in life. Attorney Jonnae Carter definitely had a ring to it. If he had to, he would be her motivator to want better in life.

Capo watched as Jonnae slept peacefully. It looked like it was one of the best sleeps she had in a long time. He slid out the bed careful not to wake her and stepped out on the balcony to return Vanessa's phone call. He sat in the lounge chair staring out to the night sky.

"So you finally decided to return my call, Ja'kahri" Vanessa answered.

"Never knew I had to Vanessa. Now what is so important that you had to blow up my phone at midnight?"

"Kahri, I want you to stop hating me. I want you to forgive me. I'm sure we can work this out together."

He laughed, "Vanessa, like I told you two years ago, we could never be again. You fucked up. You couldn't even keep your legs closed. Then you went and had the niggas baby. What you mad cuz the nigga dipped on you and left you with a baby? Remember, that's what you wanted!"

"What if I gave up my baby, then what Ja'kahri?"

He looked at the phone with a screwed face.

"Bitch, you crazy!? You're an unfit mother! You would give up your son to be with a man? You're fuckin horrible! Get the fuck off my line and don't EVER call me again! You gotta learn to be a woman before you can be a wife!"

He hung up the phone and lounged back. It was close to two a.m. The sky was clear and breezy. He felt the presence of someone behind him and was surprised to turn around and see Jonnae.

"Hey, how long you been standing there" he questioned while patting the empty space between his legs for her to sit. She walked over to him.

"Since the beginning of the conversation and no I wasn't being nosey. I just heard you yelling."

He laughed, "Nah, its cool."

"So who's Vanessa?"

He knew the question was coming.

"Vanessa was my first love and my first heartbreak. I loved Vanessa with everything in me, but two years into our relationship, I found out the feeling wasn't mutual. I found out that she was cheating and ended up pregnant by the man."

"How you know the baby wasn't yours? You just up and left without even knowing."

"When I confronted her about the cheating and pregnancy, she never denied it or said the baby was mine" he responded.

"You still never checked to see if the baby was yours?"

"If she wanted me to be a part of the child's life, she would have reached out as far as the child instead of tryna get back with me."

She nodded, "so why is she still calling two years after your relationship ended?"

"She still thinks that we have a chance of getting back together. Bitch just told me she would give up her son to be with me."

Jonnae frowned, "sad damn shame when girls will try to do anything to keep a man."

"Tell me about it, but you don't have to worry, I'm happy right where I'm at."

She smiled, "and where's that?"

He kissed her neck, "right here with you."

Chapter 19

Two weeks had passed and it was now the week of both Capo and Jonnae's birthday. Jonnae had either planned to go out and celebrate her birthday with just her and Michelle or kick back and just chill with Capo.

She had saved enough money over the past six months to buy Capo a diamond encrusted pendent. It was an eighteen karat gold pendent that said Capo. 'Capo' was completely encrusted in diamonds and each diamond was one and a half karats a piece. It cost her a pretty penny but she was always good with saving money. She was due pick it up on Thursday which was Capo's birthday. She was planning on cooking him a dinner and giving him the gift.

She'd been staying at his house for the past two weeks but she figured she would go home after his birthday. Capo couldn't lie, he was proud of her. Despite all she been through, she was still remaining strong and maintaining a B average in school.

The day of Capo's birthday arrived and Jonnae served him breakfast in bed. *I can get used to this. Waking up to her beautiful face and being catered like this,* he thought. She smiled at him, "you eat, and I'll go get ready for school."

As she was walking out the door, he called her name and she turned around to face him.

"Wassup"

He stared at her, "be my shawty."

She was a little taken aback.

"Jonnae, we've been talking to each other for seven months. My feelings for you are feelings I haven't felt since Vanessa. I know you're scared because of what Chink did and believe me, I'm still healing from Vanessa, but I believe we can treat each other better than they both treated us. We deserve better, so what you say?"

By now, he as standing face to face with her. He leaned down and kissed away her tears that were rolling down her face. She cried because she knew what he as saying was true. She slowly nodded her head.

That day, Jonnae went to school, happier than a pig in shit. She shared the news with Michelle who was just as happy. She had been waiting for the day when Capo and Jonnae made it official. The school day flew by. Jonnae told Capo that he didn't have to pick her up because she was hanging with Michelle. Real reason, she had to pick up his gift and didn't want him to see it. She walked up to the counter, "I'm picking up. It's under Jonnae Carter." The jeweler went to retrieve the piece. When the jeweler showed the piece, Jonnae and Michelle both drop their mouths.

"Oh my God, Jonnae, he's gonna love it!"

Jonnae loved it too. The jeweler gift boxed the chain and Jonnae and Michelle were on their way. Michelle dropped her off at Capo's house. He told her he wouldn't be home until about six because he was spending time with Janiylah and Jarell. That gave her two hours to prepare and cook everything even take a quick shower. She began seasoning the steaks, peeling and cutting potatoes and seasoning the asparagus for roasting. For the next hour and a half, Jonnae went to work in the kitchen. By the time she was finished, it was five thirty. She put everything in the oven to keep warm as she ran and took a shower. As she was rinsing off, she noticed Capo walk into the bathroom.

"What's good ma. Where's the food? I know you cooked something cuz I can smell it."

Jonnae looked into Capo's eyes and could instantly tell by the redness that he'd been smoking. She hated being around him when he was high, but she sucked it up cuz it was his birthday.

"Boy, go sit ya greedy munched out ass down somewhere. It'll be ready in a second."

She quickly threw on a sundress and styled her hair.

"Alright now, I'll give you five minutes but then I'm coming downstairs."

She stuck out her tongue, "fine."

She ran downstairs, and quickly plated everything as well as lit candles.

"Capo" she yelled up the stairs.

"I know I know I'm coming!"

Capo was taken aback by the candles and the dinner. On the table sat the dinner and a card.

"Wow, thanks mami." He kissed her cheek. He noticed the cake on the table and just by looking; he knew it was his favorite cake, the Death by Chocolate cake from Gregg's, his favorite munched out snack. They sat down and ate and Capo dug into his plate like it was the last meal on earth. Jonnae handed him the card.

"I couldn't find one that had the perfect words, so I found a blank one and wrote in it myself."

Capo opened the card and read it out loud.

"Ja'kahri, these past seven months have been nothing but fun. Although we are just friends, I can see something coming about. You have been there for me during my most troubling times. You never judge me based on anything I've done or have gone through. I greatly appreciate you and I hop e to make plenty of memories with you. Happy Birthday and I wish you many more. Love always, Jonnae Carter."

He leaned over and kissed her, "Thank you baby."

"I got one more gift for you, close your eyes."

She ran into the living room and grabbed the gift box out of the closet, and went back and placed it in front of him.

"Here"

He opened his eyes, looked at the box then looked at her. When he opened it, his eyes got big and his mouth dropped.

"Daaaaaaamn!!! This shit is fire! There ain't enough thank you's in the world for this shit right here ma! For real though, I appreciate it!"

She beamed with pride. His reaction was better than she anticipated. Their happy moment was interrupted by the ringing of Jonnae's cell phone. She looked at the screen and noticed that it was her mother.

"Hey ma."

"Don't 'hey ma' me! You need to come get your shit and get your fast ass outta my house."

"What! What did I do? I haven't even been there in two weeks" she exclaimed.

"You just had to fuck my man before you left, huh?"

"What the fuck!? More like his bitch ass raped me! Fuck I want with his old ugly ass?"

"Bitch, please! The way your ass sleeps around, you think I'm gonna believe you!? Just come get your shit tonight or it'll be on the sidewalk tomorrow!"

"Ma really? I sleep around? If you knew anything about

your daughter, you would know I only slept with Chink voluntarily, the other two raped me; including that piece of shit boyfriend of yours."

By now, Jonnae was in tears.

"Whatever! Just come get your shit."

Her mother hung up on her, Jonnae dropped to the floor.

"Baby girl, what happened?"

"Gary told my mom that I had sex with him. I fuckin hate him!"

He consoled her as best he could, all he seen was red. He wanted Gary so bad, he could taste it!

"Now my mom wants me out, and I have nowhere to go! Fuck, man!"

"As long as I have a house, you will always have a place to go. So if she's telling you to leave, then we'll go get your shit and you can stay here."

Every day, she became more and more grateful for Capo.

"Thanks Ja'kahri" she smiled.

"It's never a problem, BUT if you call me Ja'kahri again, there may be a problem."

They shared a laugh.

"I'm sorry I ruined your birthday night."

"You did not ruin my birthday night. I spent it with the one I wanted to spend it with."

Jonnae smiled as Capo helped her off the floor. She and Capo shared a passionate kiss. They left out the house, hand in hand and headed off to Jonnae's mother's apartment.

Chapter 20

As they pulled up, Jonnae got butterflies. Capo turned off the car and looked at her.

"You ready?"

"As ready as I'll ever be."

"Just remember, I'm right here by your side." He squeezed Jonnae's hand for assurance.

Together, they walked up to the second floor apartment. Jonnae let herself in and she instantly noticed Gary's nasty ass laying on the couch.

"Hi, Jonnae" Gary spoke.

She turned her nose up and headed to her room to pack her clothes. As she started packing, her mother showed up in the doorway.

"Take your clothes and shoes, leave everything else."

"SIKE! My iHome and television are definitely coming with me. Fuck that!"

"Jonnae chill, if she wants it, leave it" Capo stepped in.

"Ja'kahri no! I'm not leaving shit here for her to sell to get her next hit. Those were gifts!"

"From who? Your ex? Ma, I'll replace all that shit, and more so because you're not bringing shit that the last nigga bought you so you mine as well leave it."

She sucked her teeth, "Whatever!" She continued packing her clothes and sneakers. She and Capo made three trips each carrying two bags, back and forth from the apartment to the car.

"You got mad shit! Fuck you need all of this for?"

Jonnae laughed, "I don't wear half of it though."

She ran back into the house.

"Jonnae, what are you doing!? You have all your stuff!" But it went on deaf ears as she raced up the stairs. "What is this girl doing?"

On his way up the stairs, he heard a crash and then her mother yelling.

"Jonnae Myeisha Carter! Get out before I call the cops."

"And tell them what? That I trashed my own shit! Go ahead, they are gonna say there's nothing they can do, it's MY shit!" She was now in her mother's face.

Capo gently grabbed her arm, "Jonnae, mami calm down."

"Better listen to this wanna be thug if you know what's good for you" her mother spat.

"Funny, this 'wanna be thug' is more of a man that your rapist of a BOYFRIEND you got laying on ya couch! And had you not talked shit, I wouldn't have damaged my shit and you could've had it, but since you let your mouth get the best of you, have fun cleaning the shit up, TOOTLES!"

With that, she threw up the peace sign and walked out the door. Once they reached the car, Capo spoke up.

"You had to do that?"

"Yup" she snapped.

"Why!?"

"Because I fuckin did Ja'kahri! Damn, what you feel bad? You wanna go back and help her clean it? If not, then shut the hell up!"

Jonnae was tired of everyone feeling bad for her mom, fuck her! Capo pulled the car over on the side of the road.

"Listen to me! I understand you're hurt and upset, I fuckin get it. But regardless that's your fuckin mother and you only get one! Cherish it, because once they are gone, you don't get another one and it's too late to wish you spent time with them while they were here. Once she's gone, she's never coming the fuck back! Your mother has a fuckin sickness. Now she needs your help. Your brother is locked up so you are all she has. So cut the shit Jonnae, the fuck man."

Jonnae was scared because she never seen him flip the way that he just flipped on her but he was right.

"But it's okay to kick me out and keep her rapist of a fuckin boyfriend? And I'm supposed to say its okay, get the fuck outta here with that bullshit!"

"I'm not saying accept what she does, but you need to help her realize her fuck up, and not by doing the shit you just did! So whenever you're done being pissed, call her up and talk to her."

"Whatever!" Jonnae scoffed.

The remainder of the ride was silent. Jonnae just stared out the window. They pulled into the driveway and as she reached for the door, Capo grabbed her arm and stopped her.

"Nae, wait, listen, I'm sorry ma. I shouldn't have gone off like that. I just don't want you to end up like me, waiting until your mom is gone to wish you would have spent more time with her. I didn't spend much time with my mom while she was here because I took for granted that she would always be there. Yes I was always at her house, but that was because her home was my comfort place. When she was raped, I felt lost because her home was no longer safe. Someone invaded my mother's home and ripped the safety and comfort away from it. When she died, I realized I missed out on a lot. When she passed, I realized, I still needed my momma for guidance and Janiylah still does!"

She nodded and proceeded to get out the car. She grabbed her bags and made several trips to and from carries the bags. All her bags were placed in the guest room until she figured out what to do with them. By the time they made it back home, midnight was approaching. Jonnae was drained and wanted to do nothing more than take a shower and climb in bed.

"You can have my bed; I'll take the guest room."

Jonnae headed towards the shower. She found herself crying. Yes she had a tough exterior, but her mother hurt her more than she would ever know! Twenty minutes later, Jonnae was out the shower and climbing into the bed. Sleeping without Capo was odd and she tossed and turned for fifteen minutes straight. She climbed out of the bed and made her way to the guest room. She pushed the door open slightly.

"Can't sleep either huh" Capo spoke up.

"How you know?"

"Because I've been tossing and turning my damn self. Hard to break a habit you're used to."

Jonnae walked over and cuddled up in front of him. He wrapped his arms around her and within ten minutes, they were both passed out.

Chapter 21

The next day, as soon as Jonnae reached her locker, she noticed a sticky note attached to it. *Meet me here right after school, please, I promise I won't take up much of your time. –Shakeisha*

Jonnae crumbled up the noted, grabbed her books and headed off to class. She didn't know what it was, but she didn't want to be in school at all. It was Friday and her birthday was the next day, but on top of that, she couldn't get the fight with her mother out of her head. Luckily, the school day flew by. She forgot all about Shakeisha note until she noticed her standing by her locker after school.

"You got two minutes, so start talking."

Shakeisha laughed, "You're always giving someone two minutes."

"I can make it thirty seconds if you want. I suggest you start talking."

Jonnae gathered her things while she listened to Shakeisha talk.

"Jonnae, I'm so sorry. I really wish I could take it all back. It was the worst mistake ever. It didn't mean anything and it damn sure wasn't worth my friendship with you. I miss you Nae! Do you think there is any way that we can possibly work on our friendship? We've been friends for almost ten years!"

Jonnae closed her locker, "Well Keisha, you should've thought about our ten year friendship before you decided to open your legs to my boyfriend. I mean like I said before, it doesn't matter how much I complain, you're supposed to listen, not go fuckin test the waters like these other smuts! And a friendship with you? Man I don't even know about that."

"So what, you can kick it with Michelle, but not me? I mean damn Jonnae, we've been friends for so long and you're willing to throw all that away?"

"Shakeisha, that's what your problem is! You were my best friend! I trusted you with everything and you betrayed me. I can say Michelle hasn't done that, and should she ever; she will get the same treatment you get. Now, if you don't mind, I got a dress to shop for. I'll be at Karma tomorrow night. Don't say I didn't invite you!"

With that Jonnae walked off. She met Michelle outside of the school. They both jumped in the car and headed straight to the mall. They ransacked it for Jonnae's outfit. Capo had given her five stacks; no, she wasn't going to blow all of it, but she was going to blow a nice amount. After four hours of running through the stores, they decided to go down to the Chinese stores for shoes.

Jonnae returned home around seven thirty. After shopping for five hours in total, she was beat! All she wanted to do was take a shower and curl up with Capo for the night. She had a hair appointment at ten the next day and a nail appointment at twelve thirty. It was times like this where she missed Shakeisha. She was supposed to be the one shopping with her for her birthday. She missed her terribly, but she couldn't get over her fuck up.

Luckily, Capo wasn't home, so she planned on hiding her outfit in the guest room closet. She flicked on the light in the guest room and was surprised at what she saw. Both Janiylah and Tech jumped. Janiylah quickly pulled the sheet around her naked body and Tech looked like a deer caught in the headlights.

"What the fuck, Janiylah! Fuck is you doing? And Tech; really? Capo's sister!?"

Jonnae sucked her teeth. She couldn't believe what was before her eyes. Tech fuckin Janiylah? Granted, Tech was eighteen and Janiylah was fifteen, but it still wasn't something she expected.

"Jonnae please don't tell Ja'kahri" Janiylah pleaded.

Jonnae could tell that she was scared just by looking at her face. She walked out with Janiylah hot on her heels pleading with her not to say anything.

"Janiylah, what the fuck are you doing!? In your brother's house? With his boy? Really? Like come the hell on! You're fifteen girl, in this state, that is considered RAPE!"

Tech came out the room fully dressed.

"Jonnae, I'm asking, no I'm begging you, please don't tell

Ja'kahri." Janiylah was almost in tears.

"Don't tell me what" Capo asked walking through the door.

"Looks like I don't gotta say shit!" Jonnae turned to walk away.

"Since you're so quick to say shit to other people, does Capo know about you and Chink" Tech spoke up.

Jonnae stopped in her tracks and spun around.

"Know what about me and Chink?"

"Anything; or better yet, the most recent thing; you going to visit the nigga at the ACI."

Jonnae clapped her hands, "bra-fuckin-vo Tech. You just won the award for the best fuckin lie known to mankind! I haven't talked to Chink in seven months dumb ass. Since you wanna call people out, tell ya boy that you just got caught fuckin his little sister. Get yourself outta that one, asshole!" She leaned against the counter and crossed her arms across her chest.

"YOU DID WHAT!?" Capo roared. He started walking closer to Tech. Janiylah jumped in the middle.

"Ja'kahri wait..."

"Janiylah get the fuck outta my face. Tech, nigga, you're supposed to be my boy and ya fuckin my baby sister?"

"Ja'kahri, I'm not a baby anymore" Janiylah said on the

verge of tears.

"Niylah, go sit down somewhere before I smack the dog shit outta you. And go put some fuckin clothes on."

She turned and looked at Jonnae, "Thanks for nothing." She ran off crying. Jonnae felt bad because she could look in Janiylah's eyes and see that she was in love with Tech.

"Capo man, I'm sorry if you feel disrespected, but I love your sister and I care about her a great deal."

Capo stared at him, "In my house though, young? Like of all the places, I mean shit you even have your own crib, but in my shit dawg?" He shook his head, "man, just go before I lose my cool."

Tech nodded and walked out the front door. Jonnae picked up her bag and headed up the stairs.

"Uh-uh, not so fast missy. Ya still talking to this nigga?"

Jonnae was surprised, "what? No Capo, I'm not! Why would I want to go back to all the crying and fighting when I can be laughing and happy here?"

"So what the fuck is Tech talking about?"

"Hell if I know, shit I was just as surprised as you were. When I'm not at school, I'm home waiting and praying that you make it through that door."

"So where were you yesterday that you asked me not to pick you up from school?"

Jonnae couldn't believe her ears. She walked up to him and pointed to the chain around his neck, "This is what I was doing! Picking up this shit for your birthday! I really can't believe you're questioning my loyalty to you!"

"I don't know what to believe anymore."

Jonnae threw her hands in the air, "Just because your boy isn't loyal to you and is fuckin ya sister, doesn't mean I'm not loyal. I have never given you a reason to not trust me or not believe me. But I'll tell you what, I'm not gonna stand here and listen to you talk down on me. So here, you can take all this shit and return it. I don't need shit from you."

She dropped the bags down and threw the receipt and cash on the table. She took one more look at Capo and stormed out the door. She couldn't believe he was questioning her love and loyalty. Luckily, Capo only lived thirty minutes walking, outside of the city.

Chapter 22

Once Jonnae left, Capo realized he fucked up. Jonnae was right, she had never done anything or given Capo a reason not to trust or believe her. She wasn't sneaky, and she was always with him, home or at school. He lay back on the couch and stared at the ceiling. His mind was racing a mile a minute, he wanted his baby girl home yet he didn't know where she went. He heard Janiylah walk into the living room.

"Of all the niggas out here Niylah, it had to be Tech?" Capo ran his hands across his face.

"Kahri, I can't help who I love. I mean, wouldn't you want it to be a nigga you know rather than some random nigga?"

Capo looked at her, "I'd rather it be NO nigga. You're too young. I want you to get your education first. Not chasing after some nigga."

"What's the difference between me and Jonnae? She's only seventeen, I'm fifteen."

"When I met Jonnae, she had a man, but we were just friends. I respected her relationship and when she needed someone to talk to, I was there. You're my sister, so of course I'm gonna be hard on you. Yeah, Jonnae is my girl, but I'm just as hard on her. Education is number one, niggas come last. And for your info, Jonnae will be eighteen tomorrow so she's legal anyway." He stuck his tongue out at her. They both shared a laugh.

"Speaking of Jonnae, where did she go?"

Capo sighed, "Niylah I don't even know. I done let that shit Tech said get to me and I flipped on her, accusing her of still fuckin with Chink."

She slapped Capo, "really Ja'kahri? You let her fuckin go because of something that Tech said? You're such an idiot!"

Capo rubbed his cheek, "First off, hit me again, and I'm gonna knock ya ass out and swear again and I'm gonna rip your tongue out! You ain't grown!"

"Seriously Kahri, call her! You know these damn streets ain't safe and yet you let her walk around at this time of night? You're a damn fool boy! Call her and make sure that she is safe. Speaking from a woman's point of view, she'll come around when she's ready."

"I can't believe I'm taking advice from my little sister." He laughed and shook his head.

"Don't forget, I'm a younger version of Jennisse Turner!" They both laughed and Janiylah walked out the room. He picked up his phone and sent Jonnae a text. She would answer a text from him before a phone call."

Capo: bae

Nae:???

He laughed at her stubbornness.

Capo: where you at?

Nae: why? u won't believe me anyway

He sucked his teeth.

Capo: mami stop! I'm sorry, please where are you?

Nae: I'm safe, no worries, night Kahri!

Capo: Jonnae Myeisha Carter! Stop playing w/ me you know damn well I don't sleep w/out lying next to you so tell me where you at!!

Nae: haha, betta get used to it

Capo couldn't front, he was getting mad.

Capo: Ma, come on now damn! It's almost ten at night, these streets ain't safe and you know it, where you at so I can come get you with your stubborn ass!

Nae: same place you first ever saw me cry, you got 20 minutes to get here or I'm dippin.

"SAKI'S" he said out loud."

Capo: don't move, I'm comin"

He grabbed his keys and was out the door to go get his love.

Fifteen minutes later, he pulled up to Saki's. He noticed Jonnae sitting near the window staring out. He knew she saw him but she went back to eating her pizza. Capo climbed out the car and walked into Saki's straight to the booth where she was sitting.

He sat there for a good five minutes and Jonnae didn't even so much as look at him.

"You told me to come get you for you to ignore me?"

She continued to ignore him.

"Jonnae I'm sorry okay! I'm sorry. I don't believe anything that Tech said. I had a talk with Janiylah, sad to say that girl is in love with him." He shook his head. "Damn, my sister done went and fell in love and my shawty is mad and don't wanna talk to me. Damn, can a nigga catch a break anywhere?"

Jonnae looked up at him.

"In all the time I've known you, have I ever given you a reason not to trust me or believe me? Ever?"

He shook his head no.

"So how do you think I feel when I'm trying to explain something to you and you're not listening? It feels like a slap in the face when you're telling me you don't believe me."

He sighed, "I know ma, and I'm sorry, I fucked up. The nigga got caught and tried to blow up your spot! I get it, and trust me and that nigga are gonna have a talk, but bae please come home."

She looked at him, "if you're gonna constantly accuse me and not believe me then maybe we don't need to be together."

"Jonnae chill man. Until you give me a reason not to trust or believe you, then your word is all I'm taking."

She smiled and they leaned over the table and met each other half way for a kiss.

"Come on babe, let's go home." Capo reached over and grabbed Jonnae's hand and they walked out of the pizza parlor to head home.

Chapter 23

When they returned home, Jonnae went on a search for Janiylah so they could chat. She found her in the basement theatre watching *Illegal Tender* on the projection screen.

"Hey Niylah."

"Wassup Nae."

"You still mad at me?"

Janiylah sighed, "Nah, I was never mad. I just wanted to tell him in my own way."

"I'm sorry for that Niylah, but I couldn't allow Tech to try and sabotage my relationship over a bullshit ass lie," Jonnae defended.

"I understand that but damn you put me out there."

"Janiylah, one way or another, he was gonna find out. Next time tell Tech to mind his damn business and no one's business gets put on blast."

Janiylah laughed but then turned serious, "Jonnae, what am I gonna do? I love Tyron."

Jonnae's face twisted, "Who the fuck is Tyron."

"It's Tech's real name."

"Oh okay, well yeah I can tell you do love him but you have to be careful. Yes, Tech is a good guy, but he's just like Capo in a sense. They're both in the game. I worry every night about your brother. I pray all the time that I won't get a call that he's either locked up or dead. But when you deal with a hustler, those are the things you worry about. Trust me; I've been doing my brother's three year bid with him. He should be getting out in about seven months though" Jonnae said.

"You never did a bid with Chink?"

Jonnae shook her head, "Chink's never been to jail."

"So if Capo got locked up, would you do a bid with him" Janiylah asked.

"Without a doubt; unless he tells me otherwise. Believe it or not, I've loved your brother since I first laid eyes on him. He's been there for me in more way than one. I've laughed with him, cried with him, I can tell him anything and never feel like I'm being judged because of it."

"Wasn't you with Chink when you first met Ja'kahri?"

"Yeah, but I knew it was only a matter of time before Chink and I ended. Our whole relationship I had to deal with outside females. After a while, that shit gets tiring."

Janiylah laughed, "I can't see you fighting."

"Psh, girl please, ask your brother, I can hold my own."

They laughed.

"But seriously Niylah, take it from me, be with who you are happy with. If Tech makes you happy, then so be it. I stayed with chink for so long because he was all I knew. After the first year or so, I wasn't happy anymore. I loved him with everything I had; he taught me everything I know. He spoiled me to death; anything I wanted I got. But he didn't realize his money couldn't buy my love. Finding out he was fuckin someone who is supposed to be my best friend, fucked my whole head up. Funny, because that same day, was the second time I ran into your brother. He found me in the damn pizza parlor," she chuckled. "That day, we talked for hours; it also happened to be the day you were in the hospital. Despite all the bad shit that happened that day, it was also the day; I realized your brother may be who I was looking for all along. We've been tight ever since and now I'm happy we're together. Granted it's still fresh and there will be plenty of arguments, fights and disagreements but I know as long as we get through them together, we are bound to make it work."

"Aw Jonnae, that's so cute! I think you're who my brother needed though, someone who's level-headed and not a gold digger."

"Like he told me, we both have been done dirty in the past, but we deserve happiness and we can be each other's happiness."

Janiylah smiled, "thanks for the talk Jonnae. I appreciate it."

"Anytime love, anytime."

Jonnae walked back up the stairs to find Capo standing on the top.

"Eavesdropping?" Jonnae walked up to him and wrapped her arms around his neck."

"You'd do a bid with me shawty?" He leaned down and placed his forehead against hers.

"Should it come about, then yes I would." She stared into his eyes.

"I swear shawty, my feelings for you done spiraled out of control. You complete me in so many ways. I haven't felt this complete since my mom was alive. It's like she knew you were meant for me and guided you right to me."

They shared a passionate kiss; Capo scooped her up in his arms and carried her to the bedroom. As they walked in, Jonnae noticed the video that was playing on the television. She sang the chorus to Capo.

We got Hood Love, I be fussing I be screaming like its ova, then I'm longing and I'm feening just to hold ya, cuz that's how we do, you know that Hood Love is the good love, that's me and you, how you feel love, well I'm with ya, neva quit ya, now that's real love, when you ain't here then I miss ya, cuz I still love the way that we do, you know that Hood Love is the good love, that's me and you.

Capo smiled at her, "that's exactly what we have ma, Hood Love."

Jonnae smiled as Capo planted kisses all over her face; starting with her lips, then her nose, forehead and both cheeks. He slowly began descending, stopping at her breasts and teasing her nipples with his tongue. Jonnae's breathing was becoming labored; she was getting hotter by the second. Capo flicked his tongue across her nipples and softly began nibbling on them like they were Hershey kiss.

"Damn bae…" Jonnae said.

He planted kisses down her stomach. He pulled her jeans off and was kissing her pussy through her boy short underwear.

She tossed her head side to side, "Stop teasing me."

Capo smiled as he pulled her underwear down and flicked his tongue over her bulb. Jonnae's entire body shuttered.

"Shiiiiiiit" she exclaimed. She was on the verge of an orgasm.

Capo placed his entire mouth over her pussy. He slowly chewed on her bulb bringing Jonnae to her first orgasm.

"Oh shit" she yelled as her legs began to shake. She had her fingers running through Capo's hair. As he continued pleasuring her orally, Jonnae came again, hard and fast. He slurped up all her juices.

He looked up at her, with his mouth glistening with her juices. He climbed on top of her as he looked deep into her eyes. He kissed her and plunged his tongue deep into her mouth so she could taste her own juices. He moved his hand down between her legs and stuck his two fingers deep into her pussy and thumbed her clit at the same time.

"Tsssss" she hissed.

After fore-playing with Jonnae for over thirty minutes he finally pulled out his nine and a half inch tool. It was a perfect caramel color with the same smooth colored mushroom tip.

"Damn." Capo definitely had Chink beat, Chink was working with a seven maybe seven and a half inch pipe.

She tried to stop him, "wait bae..."

"Don't worry ma, I'll take it slow for you, I promise." Capo kissed her as he gently penetrated her.

"Damn shawty, ya shit is tight as fuck." Her tightness had him ready to climax early. He fought the urge. After three strokes of pain, Jonnae began feeling the pleasure.

"Faster baby." Jonnae panted.

Capo gave it to her just how she wanted it, hard and fast. He easily flipped her into different positions because she was so tiny. Jonnae was loving sex with Capo. Chink didn't do half the shit Capo did with her. He liked plain missionary whereas Capo liked everything but anal. Jonnae couldn't blame him because she wasn't with that shit either.

At one point, Jonnae thought Capo was running on an energizer battery because she came at least seven times and he hadn't busted once. She started squeezing her pussy walls.

"Whoa, wait shawty, stop doing that."

Jonnae smiled, she knew he was going to bust if she kept doing it. She squeezed once more and that was all it took.

"Ahhh." He growled.

"Fuck babe," he spoke as he released a glob of semen into Jonnae.

Jonnae was spent. Capo sexed her little ass right to sleep. She curled up next to him and was out like a light.

Chapter 24

Capo laid in the dark staring at the ceiling. He glanced at the digital clock that read twelve forty-five. He heard vibrating and reached over on the nightstand for his phone. When he looked at the screen, he noticed that it was still black. He followed the vibrating noise which led him to the floor. He pulled Jonnae's phone out of her pocket and was surprised at the name flashing across the screen.

"The fuck is this nigga calling her for?" He glanced over at Jonnae who was sleeping peacefully.

He slipped on his basketball shorts and stepped onto the balcony. He dialed the number back.

"What's good ma?" Chink answered.

"This ain't ya 'ma' homie. Fuck you calling my girl for?" Capo responded?

"What you snooping for nigga?"

"Nigga ain't no one snooping. I'm just wondering why my shawty's phone is ringing at one in the morning."

Chink laughed, "Man please!"

"'Man please' my ass, nigga. Fuck you want man? I'm tryna go back to bed with my shawty."

Chink sucked his teeth, "just tell Jonnae to return my call."

Capo laughed, "She ain't returning shit muthafucka. Fuck off her line and don't call again."

Capo ended the call before Chink could respond. He was skeptical about that phone call and it instantly made him think about what Tech had said.

"Aye, Jonnae, wake up." Capo shook her awake.

"Hmm" she moaned, half asleep. "What Ja'kahri?"

"You still fuck with Chink?"

"What? Ja'kahri, didn't we have this conversation? The fuck man," she rolled over.

"Uh-uh, if you ain't fuckin' with him, why the hell is he calling your phone; especially at one in the morning?"

She sucked her teeth, "I don't fuckin' know! Call him and ask him. Leave me the fuck alone." She threw the blanket over her head.

He pulled the blanket off her, "don't try to avoid the conversation. Why the hell is he fuckin' calling you, Jonnae?"

"What the fuck man!" Jonnae popped up, "Ja'kahri, we just had this conversation and I told you, if you were gonna

accuse me; then there is no need for us to be together. I
don't know why he fuckin' called. Maybe it's the same
reason that Vanessa is still calling you!"

Jonnae was now up and out of bed, putting on her bra and
panties as well as one of Capo's t-shirts.

"Where are you going, Jonnae?" He grabbed her arm.

She snatched her arm away, "get the fuck off me. I'm so
sick and tired of this shit Ja'kahri. I'm not Vanessa! I've
been hurt just like you have; why the fuck would I hurt you
like that?"

She walked out of Capo's room and went to the living room.
She was aggravated and tired. She grabbed the throw
blanket and lay down on the couch. Here it was, her
birthday, and she didn't even feel like doing shit anymore.
Capo pretty much ruined that. Before she knew it, she was
passed out cold.

Capo sat at the edge of his bed with his head in his hands.
He was thinking about what Jonnae said, and she was right,
she wasn't Vanessa and he needed to stop treating her like
she was.

He sat on the bed for twenty minutes before he searched
the house for Jonnae. He found her sleeping peacefully.

"I gotta stop before I end up fuckin' losing this girl," he
thought out loud. He walked over to her and kissed her
cheek lightly. "I'm sorry ma, I love you." He scooped her
and carried her back into the bedroom. He laid her down,
lay behind her and cuddled with her until he fell asleep.

Chapter 25

The next morning, Jonnae woke up to the smell of bacon frying. She looked around and noticed she was back in the bedroom. She stretched and headed to the bathroom to handle her hygiene.

She came out the bathroom and looked around for her phone. She found it on the nightstand. She quickly unlocked it and noticed over twenty unread text messages and ten missed calls. She scanned through the text messages; one from Michelle and a few other people from around the school as well as Shakeisha and Chink. Chink's message stuck out so she opened it first.

HAPPY BIRTHDAY BABYGIRL! I love you and miss you shawty. I tried calling you last night but I see you moved on and your man ain't having that. I respect it although I don't appreciate it. Anyway, Happy 18th Birthday mami! Enjoy your day and I love you!

Jonnae simply replied *Thanx Chink.*

She returned her missed phone calls. Her mother even called but when Jonnae called back, she didn't answer.

There was a call from a number she didn't recognize so she called it back.

"Yo" a man answered.

"Did someone call Jonnae from this number?"

"Happy Birthday baby girl."

Jonnae's heart skipped a beat; this couldn't be who she thought it was, "Who is this?"

"Aw, come on; don't tell me you forgot your brothers voice?"

"Boog?"

"The one and only, Nae."

"Oh my God! Where are you? When did you get out? What the fuck!"

"Slow down sis, don't worry I'm around. I'll be sure to see you today. I got out yesterday but I wanted to wait until today to tell you."

Jonnae went running out of the bedroom down to the kitchen.

"Ja'kahri, my brother..." She stopped midsentence as she stared at the male version of herself.

"Happy Birthday Jonnae."

Her mouth dropped and tears sprang from her eyes.

"Boog," she said just above a whisper.

She ran and jumped into his arms. She hugged him tight and cried. She dreamed of the day her brother came home and here he was, standing right in front of her on her eighteenth birthday. She jumped down and looked at Capo.

"You knew didn't you?"

He smiled and she playfully punched him.

"Ow kid, what was that for?" He asked rubbing his arm.

"For keeping me in the dark about my brother coming home; how did you even know how to contact one another?" Jonnae inquired.

"I wrote your brother a letter a few weeks ago, filling him in on us so that when he got out, he wouldn't be surprised that you weren't with that other nigga."

Boog spoke up, "Speaking of which, what happened between you and Chink?"

Capo rolled his eyes and Jonnae didn't miss it.

"Caught the nigga cheating with Shakeisha."

Boog's eyes popped, "wait, Keisha, Keisha? The one you grew up with?"

Jonnae nodded and Capo sucked his teeth.

"Jonnae, you were over before that."

She cut her eyes at him. "Ja'kahri, shut the fuck up."

"Excuse you?" Capo replied.

"Alright y'all damn! Jonnae, you mine as well tell me the truth. You know I'm gonna find out anyway."

She sucked her teeth, "I finally got tired of fighting with dumb broads. I broke it off and when I went to Shakeisha house to talk to her about it, I walked in on them two fucking like rabbits." She looked at Capo, "Does that sound better?"

Capo flipped her off.

"Damn, talk about grimy! That's some foul shit!" Boog stated.

"Shit I'm hungry! Where's the food at?" Jonnae asked changing the subject.

She noticed the breakfast on the table. She stuck her plate in the microwave. After they all heated up their plates, they sat down and enjoyed breakfast together. Boog asked her why she was staying with Capo and not with their mother. She and Capo looked at each other before Jonnae filled him in on what happened. He was by no means happy to hear that their mother chose a nigga over her kid. They dropped the conversation and continued eating.

"Jonnae" Capo called out.

"Wassup."

"I got something for you. Nothing too big though."

He got up and retrieved two boxes and a card.

"Like you, I couldn't find a card that had the right words so I bought a blank one and wrote in it."

Jonnae opened the card and read aloud.

"Jonnae, over the past seven months, I've grown closer to you than I have ever been close to anyone else. You have brought me nothing but happiness and I love you for that. Although it's only been a short seven months, it seems like so much longer. From the first time I seen your smooth caramel skin, I knew I had to have you. I made the decision to wait, no matter how long it took. Since getting to know you, I fell in love with you, everything about you, down to your stubbornness. Never ever doubt my love or loyalty to you because it's always gonna be GENUINE and REAL! I love you shawty, and Happy 18th Birthday! Capo."

Jonnae got up from the chair and walked over to Capo, sat on his lap and kissed him passionately; allowing their tongues to intertwine.

"Aye, Aye, I know this is your home but shit, she still is my sister, little sister at that." Boog said.

They all laughed. Jonnae picked up the longer box of the two. Inside was a fourteen karat gold chain with a name plate that read, "Capo LOVES Jonnae" with the "LOVES" in diamonds and the names in white gold.

"Aw, bae, I love you too."

Jonnae opened the last box and dropped her mouth as she lifted the key ring.

"What's this?" she asked.

"What does the key ring say?" Capo replied.

She looked at the key, "you didn't."

He smiled, "I caught the look in your eye when you first seen it so why not."

"Where is it?" Jonnae was trying to keep from screaming out loud.

"Outside"

She got up and ran out the door.

"Oh My God!" she screamed!

Chapter 26

"Bae, you really got it?" Jonnae was almost in tears. She ran around the car admiring the exterior then jumped in to view the interior.

Boog walked up behind Capo, "Damn my nigga, that bitch is clean as fuck."

Capo smiled, "She went with me to pick up my Range. She kept saying she wanted a 2010 Maxima; but what I look like allowing my girl to ride around in something that's three years old? Fuck that! When her eyes came across this, she couldn't take them off. It was like love at first sight. So now here it is, a 2013 Lexus GS 450h. I'll tell you what too, I took her for a test drive, that bitch is smooth as hell."

They both looked at Jonnae as she was in the car playing with the functions. Both Boog and Capo walked over to the car and that's when Boog noticed the License plate which read "Capos #1"

"You really want people to know your girl's driving this?"

"Yeah man, but let's see how long she'll wanna keep this before she sees something else that she wants."

Jonnae rolled down the window, "Bae thank you so much!"

She couldn't help but to cheese from ear to ear.

"Anything for my shawty; but go get dressed so we can go out."

Boog turned around and walked back to the house. Capo leaned against the car and waited for Jonnae to finish playing with the buttons of the car.

She was in love with the black interior and wood grain dashboard. She finally got out the car and stood in front of Capo between his legs. She wrapped her arms around his neck and he wrapped his arms around her waist.

"Thank you so much baby. I love it!"

He smiled, "I knew you would. I know my girl."

She admired his physique. His muscular arms bulged and his abs were noticeable threw his wife beater. His thuggish demeanor was turning her on in the worse way.

"Shawty stop, your brother is in the damn house!" Capo tried to resist.

"So what; this is your..."

Capo cut her off, "No, this is our house."

Jonnae smiled, "yeah, our house."

She kissed him and groped his dick through his pants.

"Get ya little ass in the house. Bad enough you're out here

in just a damn t-shirt and boy shorts. Don't make me fuck you up."

She winked as she walked away, "maybe I want you too."

"Jonnae I'm gonna kick your ass. Go on girl!" He smiled as he watched her walk into the house.

Damn, I fall more and more in love with that girl every day Capo thought.

He followed her inside the house and to the bedroom. He closed the bedroom door and striped as he followed the sound of the shower to the bathroom. When he opened the door, he seen Jonnae with her eyes closed as she wet her hair under the shower head. He slowly pulled the shower door back and stepped in. Jonnae peeked out of one eye.

"Ja'kahri, don't start."

Capo pushed Jonnae's breast together and began sucking on her nipples.

"Damn," Jonnae hissed.

Capo dropped his hand down to her pussy and began fingering her and thumbing her clit. His mouth moved from her breast to her lips. He then began planting kisses down her body until he reached her pot of gold.

"What are you doing?" she asked, out of breath.

He covered her clit with his mouth and began sucking and biting on it softly.

"Damn Ch..." She caught herself. Hopefully Capo didn't hear her, but little did she know he did.

Why the fuck am I thinking about Chink she thought.

Capo quickly made her cum, washed his body and got out the shower. To say he was pissed, was an understatement. How the fuck could she be thinking about the next nigga as he's sitting there eating her pussy?

"Maybe I moved too fast and should've given her more time to get over him" he said out loud.

Jonnae stood behind him crying. She loved Capo and wanted to be with him, but after that, she wasn't so sure whether or not he would believe her.

"Ja'kahri" she called.

He ignored her; his heart was hurting.

"Baby, talk to me."

"Jonnae, are you over him?" Capo questioned.

"Yes Ja'kahri. I promise you, I love you and want to be with you."

"Are you sure about that?" He lifted his head out of his hands. "Because if not, we can end this right now; I'm not up for being hurt again Jonnae."

She dropped to her knees in front of him, "Ja'kahri Turner, I give you my word, I want no one but you. I'm so sorry."

She broke down crying because she was truly afraid that she was going to lose him after that stunt. He grabbed her face and wiped her tears. He softly kissed her lips.

"Stop crying ma."

"I'm sorry, I really am sorry!" Jonnae sniffled.

"Shh, it's cool; just don't let it happen again, okay?"

She smiled and nodded as she leaned in to kiss him again.

"Go ahead and get dressed, so we can go. Oh and your outfit you bought for tonight, yeah you're getting something else."

She frowned, "Why?"

"Cuz I'm not a fan of it. I mean you can keep it but tonight you're wearing something else."

"That's a waste of money Capo."

He looked at her sideways, "Jonnae since when did money ever become an issue?"

She just started at him.

"Exactly, now get dressed."

He started walking out but then stopped again, "oh, last thing, your hair appointment is at two now."

She shook her head and laughed.

Jonnae, Capo and Boog spent two hours shopping and instead of Jonnae getting one outfit, she ended up walking out with four. Neither she nor Capo could come up with just one that they both liked.

"Aye bae, you and Boog head over to the food court, I'm gonna go check and see if Foot Locker got these sneakers I been looking for."

Jonnae nodded as her and Boog made their way to the food court.

"Boog? Is that you?" They heard a female say.

They both turned around and seen Shakeisha. Boog gave Jonnae a look that said, "Don't start."

"What's good Keisha?" He leaned in and hugged her.

"Oh my God, when did you get out?"

"Yesterday."

"Wow, you look good." She looked over to Jonnae, "Hey Jonnae."

She rolled her eyes and walked away.

"Keisha, why you do her like that; that's supposed to be your best friend, we family, you don't do that."

She dropped her head, "Boog, I've been apologizing for seven months. She acts like I don't even exist."

"How you expect her to act Keisha? Look what you did. You crossed the line."

"I know I fucked up Boog! I miss her terribly. Do you think you can talk to her for me?"

Boog sighed, "I'll try but you know Nae is stubborn. Ain't no telling if she'll even listen."

They both noticed Jonnae and Capo walking towards them.

"I see she got with Capo huh." Shakeisha stated.

Boog whipped his head towards her, "How you know him?"

"Relax; I was with her when they met."

"Hm, okay. Well stay up Keisha, I'll see you around."

They hugged and went their separate ways.

"Who Boog talking too?" Capo questioned.

"Shakeisha."

Capo laughed, "Wow."

They finished their last minute shopping and left so Jonnae would make it to her nail appointment. She was fifteen minutes late but they still took her because she always tipped well. An hour and a half later, she was walking out the door and heading to her hair appointment. A simple wash and blow dry was all she needed. By the time she was finished, it was close to four thirty.

"I'm going to take a nap," Jonnae stated as they pulled up to the house.

She kissed Capo, hugged Boog and made her way into the house. They watched as she walked into the house.

"She's beautiful," Capo spoke.
"Yeah, Nae is my world bruh. As long as you keep her happy, we'll be good."

"Oh most definitely Boog; she is my happiness. Like I told her, I haven't felt this complete since my mom passed."

Boog nodded, "Do me a favor though, try to keep her away from the drug life."

"I would never place her there, but I don't hide anything from her. She knows what I do, but I don't bring her around my dealings. But should anything happen to me, she'll know how to maintain for herself. She knew all that though before we even got together. Everything I own is legit though because I have very successful businesses out of state."

Boog nodded and respected Capo even more.

"Come on; let's cruise around the city while the beauty queen gets her rest."

They both laughed and walked to the garage to pull out Capo's newest baby, the Corvette.

Chapter 27

Boog and Capo cruised around the city as Boog took in the scenery. Two and a half years later, some shit looked different while other shit looked the same.

"Look man, I'm fresh out, with little cash and a record. Help a brotha out." Boog said to Capo.

Capo picked up on what Boog was saying right off the back. He nodded, "I got you Boog, no worries. But since you're fresh out, enjoy your freedom a little bit. I'll give you some cash to hold you over for a few weeks and next week we'll start talking business. Until then, enjoy your freedom."

Boog dapped Capo up, "Good look man, I appreciate it. And any cash you give me, I'm paying it back. I don't do well will just taking from people."

"Understandable and I feel you on that too. Not a problem either, you're family so of course I'm gonna look out for you."

They cruised around for another hour before they headed back to the house.

"Aye, I'm about to go crash for a little bit, the keys to the Beemer are on the hook. Feel free to take it but be careful with my baby." Capo joked.

"I got you. Why can't I take the Lex?"

Capo laughed, "Yeah right, let that car out of Nae's sight and watch her go ballistic."

"I'm only joking my nigga." They dapped each other up again as Capo headed upstairs and Boog headed out the door.

Boog planned on going back to the hood to see if he could catch up with KB and Chiefy. He also had to pay his mother a visit. He wasn't happy about the shit that Jonnae had told him. He and Capo had secretly spoken about it, and Capo still wasn't happy about it, but Jonnae begged him not to do anything on the sake of her mother. Capo promised, but Boog never made that promise.

Twenty minutes later, he pulled up in front of his mother's apartment building. He walked up to the second floor and slowly approached apartment 2B. His heart raced, he hadn't seen his mother and didn't know how bad her condition was. He raised his hand to knock, when suddenly the door opened. He looked at the lady standing before him and due to the lightness of her eyes and the length of her hair, he knew this lady standing before him with the sunken cheeks, was his mother. Her lips were dry, ashy and cracked, but this was Rita Carter, his mother.

"Hey momma," Boog spoke.

Her hand flew over her mouth, "Jonathan?"

"The one and only."

Tears instantly sprang to her eyes.

"Oh my God, my baby! Momma missed you so much." She hugged him tightly, "Come on in, excuse the mess, I haven't had the chance to straighten up yet."

"Rita, I thought you were going to the store." A gruff voice asked coming from the bathroom.

Gary's eyes locked with Boog's and from the stare, Gary caught a chill. Before him, he saw a male version of Jonnae.

"Gary, this is my son Jonathan, Jonathan this is Gary." Rita introduced.

Gary reached his head out for a handshake from Boog, "What's up Jonathan."

Boog looked down at his hand and back up to Gary, "it's Boog to you."

Gary cleared his throat, "Uhm, Rita are you going to the store?"

Before Rita could answer Boog stepped in, "No, you are."

Rita stepped in, "No Jonathan, it's okay, I'll go."

Boog looked at her, "No ma, like I said, Gary here can go. Plus we need to talk."

Gary nodded and proceeded to grab a jacket to walk to the store. Soon as he walked out the door, Boog started in on his mother.

"Who's that?" he questioned.

"My boyfriend."

"Is he the reason you decided to throw my sister out on her ass like she wasn't shit?" He wasted no time getting straight to the point.

"Jonnae is the reason why she ain't here."

"And how's that ma?" Boog now sat on the coffee table directly across from his mother.

"Ask her."

"I did, but I want to hear it from you."

Rita sighed, "She slept with Gary."

"And who told you that?"

"He did!"

"And you believed him over your daughter?"

"Shit, what else was I supposed to believe? I've heard a few people say she sleeps around."

"Ma, are you fuckin' kidding me? She been with Chink for almost three years and that's the only muthafucka she has been with! And regardless of what you heard, that's still your daughter and you're always supposed to be there for her! Why not ask her what happened rather than jump down her throat and jump to conclusions!"

Rita had tears in her eyes, "she disappeared for two weeks straight."

"Did you ever wonder why? Did you ever call and find out why she hadn't come home?"

She sucked her teeth, "You were locked up so how would you know anything that is happening out here?"

"Because unlike you, I care about Jonnae and I call her every day to check on her."

"I'm supposed to believe he raped her?" Rita questioned.

"You damn sure shouldn't have kicked your daughter out and kept him here. Jonnae never EVER gave you problems, and you turned your back on her. For God's sake ma, she's your damn kid! That's foul momma!"

Rita was in full blown tears, "How the fuck you think I feel knowing my man has a fuckin' crush on my seventeen year old daughter? She had to go!"

"By you knowing that, that should have been more reason for you to get rid of his ass, not Jonnae! She didn't even do anything."

Little did Boog know, Rita regretted the decision she made every day. She felt like she needed Gary because he fed her drug and alcohol habit. At that moment, Gary walked through the door.

"Ma, let me tell you this, if I come back here again, and this nigga is still here, you mine as well write me out of your life."

"I guess she'll be writing you off then because I ain't going anywhere lil nigga."

Boog stepped up in Gary's face, "Muthafucka you can either walk out of here on your two feet or on a fuckin' stretcher. That is your choice, but I can make the decision for your punk ass if you'd like. On the sake of my momma, I won't body your ass, but if you even think about my sister again, I can't promise that I won't do something next time."

Boog began walking out the door and stopped in his tracks, "Momma, remember what I said, Gary or me and Jonnae. The choice is yours."

He turned and walked out. He jumped in the Beemer and headed to see if he could find Chiefy and KB. As he was riding up the block, he recognized a familiar face; well a familiar ass. From the back, he could see that she put on a few pounds but it was in all the right places. He pulled up on the side of her and she had to do a double take.

"Boog; is that you?"

"The one and only mami," he flashed his smile.

He got out the car and walked over to the passenger's side of the car and leaned against it.

"Oh my God," Kittie squealed as she hugged him tight.

"How are you? Damn you look good!"

"I'm alright, two and a half years is a long ass time. Think you can help a brother out?"

Kittie instantly picked up on what he was asking for.

"Haven't I always looked out for you in the past?" she questioned sexily.

"Yeah, you do, where we going?"

"My crib is about two blocks away, we can go there." Kittie replied.

Boog agreed, they jumped in the car and headed to Kittie's where she fucked and sucked the shit out of Boog for the next three hours.

Chapter 28

Back at the house, Jonnae had just woke up from her nap. She rolled over and smiled when she noticed that Capo was lying next to her. She kissed his cheek and got up to go to the bathroom. When she came back out, she heard her phone ring. Capo rolled over and grabbed it before she did.

"Jonnae, why this nigga still calling you?"

She shrugged, "Answer it and find out."

Capo just stared at her as he answered the phone.

"Yo."

Chink sucked his teeth, "Man put Jonnae on the phone."

"Fuck I tell you about calling her?"

"NIgga just put her on the phone."

Capo removed the phone from his ear.

"Jonnae, tell this nigga to stop fuckin calling. I'm not playing!" Capo spoke through clenched teeth. He tossed the phone to her.

"Tell him," he said.

She nodded, "Yes Chink?"

"Damn, ol' boy won't even let you have a conversation with a friend?"

"Chink, you're not a friend! You're my ex; a perfect EXample of what not to date again. An EXperience that I never want to go through again! Make this the last time you call me." She hung up.

"Next time the nigga calls, I'm gonna fuck him up!"

"Bae, calm down. He's only doing the same thing that Vanessa's doing. Working with a hope and a prayer," she replied.

"Call it whatever the fuck you want, just remember what the fuck I said."

"You can lose ya attitude with me cuz I didn't do shit!"

"Yeah whatever."

"Again, Ja'kahri, with the accusations, cut the shit! I'm right where I wanna be, with whom I wanna be with." She walked up to him, "and that's right here with you."

He smiled and leaned over to kiss her. "I love you girl," Capo said, looking into her eyes deeply.

"I love your sickening ass too."

He really wished his mother could have met her. She would have fallen in love with her.

"What you thinking about, love?" Jonnae asked.

"About how I wish you could've met my mother. She would have loved you, all the way down to your stubbornness."

Jonnae chuckled, "I love her for creating such a handsome yet sickening ass son."

"Ha ha ha, very funny asshole," Capo said as he mushed her. She slapped him and went running through the house with Capo hot on her heals.

She laughed as she thought about how childish they looked but fuck it, they were having fun. She slid across the floor and landed on the couch. Capo caught her and began tickling her. She laughed uncontrollably.

"Bae stop, I can't breathe. I'm gonna piss myself," Jonnae yelled through laughs.

"Nope, you should have thought about that before you decided to hit and run."

Capo continued tickling her and Jonnae could not stop laughing; she had tears rolling down her cheeks.

"Capo, stop please, I'm sorry," she continued laughing.

Neither of them heard Boog walk into the house. "Aye man, what you doing to my sister?"

"Tickling her ass since she wanna hit people and run."

"Ja'kahri stop," she couldn't stop laughing and both her stomach and cheeks were hurting from laughing. "I'm gonna kick you in your nuts."

That got his attention, "Oh no, I need those. I have to make a Ja'kahri Jr. and a daddy's little princess," he said as he cupped his dick.

"For a second, I thought you were hitting my sister, I almost flipped." Boog said.

"Nah man, I would never do that. Shit she's the one doing all the hitting."

"Ahh shut up you punk!" Jonnae joked.

"Keep talking shit Jonnae, and I'm gonna tag your ass."

"Yeah and I'm gonna help him," Boog chimed in.

Jonnae's jaw dropped, "Boog, you're supposed to be on my side! You're my brother you're just his brother in law."

Boog shrugged, "I don't say the 'in-law' and you've always had a mouth so I know how he feels."

Boog and Capo dapped each other up.

"Fuck both y'all punks." Jonnae yelled. She looked at the clock and noticed it was after nine.

"Y'all go get your feminine asses ready, I'm tryna be at

Karma by eleven. And you two are worse than bitches when it comes down to getting dressed." She laughed at her own statement.

"Yeah whatever nigga, but baby, you gotta do my braids over," Capo yelled as she was walking up the stairs.

"See, I told you, worse than a bitch."

"Shut up. Grab the comb and Jam whlle you're up there."

Jonnae flipped him off.

"Keep fuckin' with me Jonnae," Capo laughed.

Boog chuckled, "Well while you two love birds fight over who's getting their hair done, I'm jumping in the shower."

"No one cares Boog," Jonnae said while walking down the stalrs.

"Jonnae, sister or no sister, birthday or no birthday, I can and will fuck your little ass up."

They all laughed as Capo and Jonnae headed to the living room and Boog headed to the bathroom. Jonnae sat on the couch and Capo sat between her leqs. She took out his two braids that were already in and proceeded in styling.

"I love you," Capo randomly said.

"I love you too," and Jonnae meant it; she truly loved Capo.

Chapter 29

Ten minutes later, Jonnae finished Capo's two braids. As she greased his scalp, she asked him, "Have you ever thought about cutting your hair?"

"Yeah, when my mom first passed, I was gonna cut it because she was the only one who braided it for me. I didn't cut it because Janiylah learned to braid and now I have you so there is no reason for me to cut it." He smiled and showed his perfect set of thirty-two's and his dimples.

"I love your smile," Jonnae stated.

"Why?"

"Because, you have the perfect set of teeth and your dimples just set it off. It's almost perfect." She laughed.

"You're so corny kid. Who says that?"

She mushed him, "Shut up!"

"Aye, unless you want me to tickle your ass again, I suggest you keep your hands to yourself."

Jonnae threw her hands up in defense, "Nope, you win; I'm not hitting you anymore."

They both shared a laugh, "I thought you would see it my way," Capo joked.

"Hey, let's practice saving water." Jonnae suggested.

"Whatever floats your boat lil mama, just don't try anything."

"What? How you gonna say whatever floats my boat and then say don't try nothing? Hm, you are something else," she said in her best Kevin Hart voice.

Capo busted out laughing, "You're stupid kid. Let's go because you know you're gonna take forever to get dressed."

"Shut up."

They headed to the shower together. Fifteen minutes later, they jumped out the shower. It was ten of ten; Karma was ladies free before eleven.

As Capo was digging in his closet for something to wear, Jonnae noticed something glistening. She recognized it as a hidden door.

"Bae," she called.

"Yeah, ma?" he answered, his back still facing her.

"What's the door for?"

He looked down and noticed that she was talking about his emergency door.

"Emergency exit."

"Where does it lead too?" Jonnae inquired.

"It leads to a room that has televisions that show the areas of the house with cameras. Inside, there is another door which leads to the garage ceiling. You can move a certain tile and drop to the floor for a clean escape."

"Hm." Jonnae nodded.

"Incase anything happens, that's your way out. There are emergency drugs, money, guns, and spare car keys. Ever notice that I don't lock the bedroom door?"

She nodded; she always wondered why he didn't.

"That's because when you do, the projection screen drops and shows all the views of the house with cameras. The bedroom door is bulletproof but that doesn't mean it can't be knocked down. But remember that, just in case. You never know, everyone accumulates at least one hater a day." he chuckled.

"I got it babe," Jonnae replied.

A half an hour later, they were all in the living room looking fresh. Jonnae was dressed in a black thigh high, strapless Versace dress. She loved it, especially because it made her already plump ass look even better. Her D-cup breast was on display. Capo actually took a good look at Jonnae in her dress and instantly wanted to rip it off her, bend her over the couch and fuck her right there. He had to contain himself and get his 'little guy' under control.

Capo wore a crisp pair of True Religion jeans, a fresh white V-neck shirt with a True Religion button up over it. On his feet was the Olympic Jordan 7's; fresh and thuggish. He threw on his Fendi shades just to offset the outfit.

Boog also wore True Religion jeans, with a black V-neck with the black and gold Jordan 7's from the Olympic gold package. Although he was locked up, the last year of his bid, Jonnae made sure to stock up on all the up-to-date gear.

As they got outside to jump in the car, Boog stopped Capo and asked if he could take the Beemer.

"You know Ms. Show Off is taking her Lexus."

"And you know this man." Jonnae did her best Chris Tucker impersonation.

"Yeah, man, go ahead but be careful." Capo said.

"No doubt, good lookin' bruh."

Capo jumped in the passenger's side of the Lex while Jonnae jumped in the driver's seat.

"Aye ma tonight is your night. Forget all the drama and bullshit, and enjoy yourself."

She smiled, "I got you bae."

"Oh and another thing, you better stay within eye sight of me."

She frowned, "Why?"

"With that short ass dress on, I'll end up killing a muthafucka. I'm tryna enjoy myself with you, but I'll fuck a nigga up if I have too."

Jonnae laughed, "They can holla all they want; I know who I'm going home with at the end of the night."

Chapter 30

They pulled up to Karma and noticed the line wrapped around the corner.

"Uh, if you ever think I'm standing in that long ass line in these six inch heels, you're fuckin' insane."

"Jonnae, really? Money talks ma, plus you got VIP, no line. Straight like that!"

Jonnae parked in the far corner so no one would ding or dent her new baby. She saw the stares and whispers when she pulled up. Her and Capo got out the car and walked hand in hand to the front of the line. She spotted Michelle and grabbed her out of line. She then noticed Tayla, she just rolled her eyes and kept walking.

"Bitch, thinks she's fuckin' better than someone. Watch that ass end up right back at the end of the line," Tayla spoke to her friend.

Jonnae heard her comment and so did Capo, he grabbed her hand tighter and whispered, "Ignore her, remember what I said ma."

Jonnae, Michelle and Capo made their way to the front of the line. Capo dapped up the bouncer.

"What's good Cap?"

"Shit man, out here celebrating my shawtys birthday," he answered pointing to Jonnae.

"You're the one pushing that fly ass whip. What you rent it for your birthday?" the bouncer asked.

Before Jonnae could answer, Capo jumped in, "Man, don't insult me like that. You know damn well I don't rent shit. She own that muthafucka. Don't believe me, check the tags."

"My bad, my dude. Go enjoy yourself; Happy Birthday beautiful."

"Thank you."

Tayla's mouth dropped as she heard the conversation between the bouncer and Capo. She was even madder when she watched Jonnae walk straight in the club without having to wait in the long ass line like she did.

When Jonnae, Capo and Michelle made it inside, they were surprised to see how packed it was. They walked straight over to VIP which had a banner on the wall behind it that said 'Happy Birthday Jonnae'. Jonnae noticed buckets of ice with Champagne bottles in them.

"Don't even think about it," Capo whispered.

"What?"

"You mine as well get your eyes off the bottles, you ain't drinking. You got a car to drive home."

"Capo, I don't drink; and even if I did," she dangled the keys in his face, "you would just drive home."

She smiled and he just smirked. They kicked it in VIP for a little while. A few people came over and wished her a happy birthday. After fifteen minutes of sitting in VIP staring around the club, Jonnae and Michelle made their way to the dance floor. Jonnae felt someone tap on her shoulder and when she turned around, she noticed it was Chink.

"Happy birthday, ma."

"Thanks." She turned to walk away when Chink grabbed her arm.

"Wait..."

"Chink just stop."

Capo was watching the whole ordeal take place and he wasn't a happy camper. He would wait a few more minutes and if he looked like he wasn't trying to budge, then he would step in.

At that time, one of her favorite songs began to play. As the words began to play, she looked dead into Chink's eyes and began singing with Keyshia Cole.

I admit that you almost had me, I admit I was almost crazy, had me thinking 'bout calling that bitch that night, let her know where she can come and meet me, but it's cool imma be a lady, she think she cute but she don't faze me, and if you knew about all of this good lovin you'll be missing out on, you wouldn't have played me, can't say I'm not hurt, I'll be damned if I'm broken, what we had is now hers, let her know she can have it.

Jonnae was almost in tears as Keyshia Cole sang her heart out. She headed for the nearest exit, she needed fresh air. Her emotions were everywhere. Michelle and Capo both followed her.

"Nae, what's wrong?" Michelle questioned.

She sighed, "I'm good Chelle, thanks."

"You sure?"

She nodded.

"Aight then," Michelle turned around and walked inside.

Jonnae took a few deep breaths to recompose herself.

"You good ma?"

"Yeah, I'm alright."

He walked up to her and hugged her tight; he knew that whenever she was ready to discuss what was bothering her, she would.

After being outside for a few minutes, Capo guided her back inside. When they got to the front entrance, they noticed Boog being harassed.

"Aye, what's going on?" Capo asked.

"He ain't tryna let me in talking about they at capacity." Boog explained.

Jonnae walked up to Boog and looped her arm through his, "he's my brother so he's getting in."

They walked in the club together.

The bouncer looked at Capo, "You got a feisty one on your hands huh?"

Capo chuckled and nodded.

Chapter 31

Jonnae was enjoying herself. She stayed on the dance floor for most of the night. Capo even joined her a few times, but most of the time he just scoped from VIP. Capo got up from VIP and made his way to the DJ booth.

"Hey everybody, can I have you attention for a quick second," Capo spoke into the microphone.

Everyone looked towards the stage.

"What is he doing?" Jonnae mumbled.

"I just wanna wish my shawty a happy birthday! I hope you're enjoying yourself. To see the smile on your face is priceless. Remind me to get double insurance on that Lexus though."

Everyone laughed.

"Nah, but for real, I love you ma, and I'm glad I can celebrate your birthday with you. Remember, it's always..."

"Jonnae and Ja'kahri against the world," they said in unison.

"I love you shawty." Capo finished.

Everyone clapped and made way as Capo and Jonnae made their way to each other.

"I love you too papi." Jonnae said as they shared a kiss.

Capo stayed on the dance floor with Jonnae. She glanced over and noticed Boog talking to a chick with pants so tight; it looked like the seams were going to bust. She laughed.

"What's so funny?" Capo asked.

"Boog's lady choice."

He turned around and noticed what she was talking about, "Leave him alone."

The DJ came over the microphone.

"Excuse me, I'm sorry to stop your partying because I know ya'll are enjoying yourselves. I just have one song request from Capo to Jonnae."

Jonnae looked at Capo as "Ride or Die" by Ace Hood and Trey Songz blared throughout the club. Capo looked at her as he sang along with Trey Songz.

Even though I'm in the streets, you know exactly what I do, when I chase this paper, you ain't gotta wait for me to bring it back home to you, cuz I ride or die, girl we gon' be good, and if you ride or die, we gon' make it out this hood

"I promise you shawty, I'm gonna take you away from these streets and treat you like the queen you are." They sealed the deal with a kiss.

Before they knew it, it was three am and the club was letting out. Jonnae's feet were killing her, so Capo told her to wait as he went and got the car. While she was waiting, Tayla felt the need to bump into her as she walked by.

"Tayla, what the fuck is the deal with you girl?" Jonnae asked. She was tired of this bitch.

"YOU are my problem, Ms. Jonnae Carter."

"Me? What the fuck have I ever done to you?"

"You walk around like you're better than someone, when you really ain't shit. What because you got a man with money, you think you're the shit?"

Jonnae chuckled, "See Tayla, that's where your problem is. I NEVER thought I was better than anybody, but it's obvious that YOU think I'm better than somebody. I mind my business, go to school and go home. I don't brag about the shit I have or the shit I can get. Money don't mean that much to me."

"JONNAE!" Tayla and Jonnae both turned their head in the direction of the voice. That's when they noticed Capo was standing outside of the car.

"Let's go," he spoke in a stern voice.

Jonnae walked over to the car and headed towards the passenger's side.

"No, driver's side; this is your shit not mine."

Jonnae rolled her eyes; Capo just had to make it known that the Lexus was Jonnae's. She switched her shoes from her heals to her flip flops. They got in the car and she peeled off. She didn't want Capo to say anything but she knew that he was going too.

"Fuck was that shit back there?" Capo questioned.

"I asked her a question, she gave me an answer, and I clarified shit. Nothing serious." Jonnae answered nonchalantly.

"Arguing outside of a fuckin' club though? Come on ma, stop stooping down to the level of these birds!"

"I wasn't arguing with her, but okay. I don't feel like arguing about it."

The remainder of the ride was silent. They pulled up to the house; Jonnae went inside and headed straight for the bedroom. She washed her face, wrapped her hair, stripped out of her dress and laid on the bed. She was out like a light. She never heard her phone ring nor did she feel Capo climb in the bed with her.

Chapter 32

As the months went by, Jonnae and Capo grew closer. She was in school faithfully and was doing well. She decided, after graduation, she would take general studies at the Community College and then transfer out of state. Capo backed and supported her.

Capo and Boog became tight. After staying with Jonnae and Capo for a few months, Boog had stacked up enough money to get his own spot. Capo was often there, but mainly for business. Well, that's what Jonnae thought anyway. Jonnae trusted Capo enough that he wouldn't do anything.

Their first Christmas together was amazing. It was just Jonnae, Janiylah, Capo, Jarell, and Boog. They were their own mini family. Jonnae got a ring from Capo, not an engagement ring, but a promise right. Jonnae bought Capo a pair of diamond earrings. Jonnae bought Boog sneakers, Janiylah got cash from both Capo and Jonnae and Jarell didn't know what he wanted so Capo promised to take him on a shopping spree.

The New Year was just Jonnae and Capo. They brought it in together, kissed under the mistletoe and everything. Jonnae loved the way her relationship with Capo was going.

Chink still called every now and again trying to at least be friends with Jonnae. She always ignored him or answered with one word answers. Sometimes she missed Chink but when she thought back to all the bullshit, she was more than glad she let his ass go.

One night, Capo and Jonnae were lying in bed watching bed watching *Baby Boy*, which happened to be one of Jonnae's favorite movies. Capo laughed at her as she repeated the movie and even acted like Yvette.

"Capo, if you ever do me how Jodi did Yvette, I will hurt you."

"But he loved her and she knew she was wifey."

Jonnae scrounged her face, "So that makes it okay for him to have a baby by someone else? And fuck whoever he wants because they 'broke up'? Please don't make me punch you."

Capo laughed, "Chill gangsta; don't worry, only babies I'm having are coming right out of here." He grabbed Jonnae's pussy.

"Yeah they better, or it's gonna be World War III. Believe that!"

They continued watching the movie together. Jonnae fell asleep before the end of the movie. Capo moved her so she went from lying on his lap to lying flat on the bed. Just as he was about to get comfortable to call it a night, his phone rang. Looking at the clock, he saw that it was a quarter past midnight. He checked the screen and seen Boog's name flash across it.

"What's good bruh?" he answered.

"I need you to swing by my crib now."

"What's the emergency?"

"Can't say too much over the phone, but just know I got some info you might like to know in regards to who's been skimming off your shit."

"Say no more; I'm on my way."

They disconnected and Capo quickly dressed in basketball shorts and his black champion hoodie. He thought about waking Jonnae to tell her he was leaving but decided against it. He would be back before she even realized he was gone.

He ran outside and decided to take her Lexus since it was the only car that wasn't in the garage. He jumped in, and peeled off in route to Boog's bachelor pad.

An hour later, Jonnae was woken up from her sleep.

"What the fuck was that?" Jonnae thought and jumped up as the heard the front door of her house being kicked in. Capo had always told her to be prepared for a day such as this. She then remembered, Capo didn't move, so she glanced to the opposite side of the bed and realized he wasn't there. "Where the fuck did he go?" she thought to herself. Her instincts told her things were going to get ugly if she didn't do something quick. She heard the intruders messing up her living room and kitchen. She quickly locked her bulletproof bedroom door which automatically caused a projection screen to drop and the cameras that were placed in her house to show the footage of her living room and kitchen. It brought tears to her eyes to see her living room and kitchen a total mess.

She got herself together and ran to her closet, which held the door to a smaller room that contained emergency guns, clothes, money, drugs and anything else that could be needed. This room also had TVs that showed every room in her house. She constantly wondered, "Where the fuck is Capo?" As she glanced back to the television screens, she realized that the intruders were no longer in the living room and kitchen but they were heading up the stairs in her direction.

She threw on an all-black sweat suit and a pair of black tennis shoes as fast as she could. She grabbed her emergency hand bag that she kept in the hidden room and started throwing all the stacks of money and a few guns in the bag. She looked back at the screens again and realized the Intruders were heading towards the bedroom door. She started panicking but tried to remain under control because if she panicked, it could cause her life. She ran to the other door In her closet, which led to a tile in the garage ceiling. Once she dropped onto the garage floor as quickly and quietly as possible, she hoped she had enough time to get the garage door open and flee the house before the intruders made it back downstairs.

She quickly decided on taking Capo's Corvette over the Range Rover, the seven series Beemer and the C-class Mercedes. She quickly pressed the button on her car remote to open the garage door. That was the one thing she hated about the house, the garage door made so much noise as it opened and moved slow. The Corvette was started and the doors were locked. She felt a little safer in the cars because all of them cars were bulletproof all around.

As soon as the garage door opened enough for the Corvette to slide out, the door that separated the house from the garage went flying open. Jonnae stomped on the gas pedal as she glanced in her review mirror into a pair of eyes she once told herself she would never forget. She couldn't believe the person who once owned her heart and soul was the same person who ransacked her home.

Chapter 34

As Jonnae drove, she couldn't get those eyes out of her head. She quickly dialed Capo's number and it constantly rang and went to voicemail. She hung up and called again. She called five times back to back until he answered and as soon as he did, she laid into his ass.

"Where the fuck are you and why aren't you answering your phone?"

"Whoa, slow down! I'm at Boog's. Where are you and why does it sound like you're driving?"

"I'm on my way to you and because," she felt tears beginning to form, "someone broke into the house."

"WHAT!?" Capo roared. "Ma, where are you?"

"I just pulled up outside of Boog's."

Capo hung up and ran out the door to get Jonnae. When she seen him, she fell into his arms and broke down.

"Shh, ma it's okay; I got you." Capo assured her.

Jonnae could not stop thinking about those eyes. She couldn't believe he stooped that low. Was he trying to send Capo a message? Or better yet, send her a message? She was scared now.

After she calmed down, they walked up to Boog's apartment.

"Ma, did you do exactly what I told you to do?

She nodded.

"Did you see anything on the cameras?"

She shook her head no, "They had on masks."

"They? So there was more than one?"

She nodded, "There was two."

"Did you notice anything about them?"

Should she tell him that the eyes she saw belonged to Chink? That he was the one who broke into their home? She knew that if she told Capo, he would go after Chink and most likely kill him. She couldn't have that on her conscious.

She shook her head, "No, I got out as fast as I could."

Capo didn't believe her because it took her too long to answer.

"Boog, put a word out on the street, fifty grand for any information leading me to the muthafuckas that broke into my shit. In the meantime, I'm running to the house to get some last minute shit before I call the insurance company. Ma, you stay here."

She nodded, but she was still very shaken up. Every

question was floating through her head. "What did Chink want?" She had to find out. It wasn't a smart idea, but she was going to do it anyway.

After Boog and Capo left, Jonnae climbed into Boog's bed and noticed she had a text message.

Chink: U still gunna ignore me?

It was from Chink.

Nae: I'm not ignorin you; what is it u want?

She waited for his reply.

Chink: I just wanna see u and talk to u, u so wrapped up into this nigga, u ain't even tryna hear shit

She rolled her eyes.

Nae: See me for what Chink? U put me in danger; why the fuck would u break into our house!?

She knew she should have just ended the conversation.

Chink: Just meet me, I'll explain everything, plus I didn't know u were there, your car wasn't outside...

She sucked her teeth.

Nae: That doesn't mean shit! Smh

Chink: Nae, just meet me, then if u want me to leave u alone after that, I will, just please gimme a few

minutes.

Jonnae said a quick prayer, "Lord, please protect my relationship."

Nae: Meet you where?

Chink: Hilton – downtown, room 504

Jonnae sighed, she knew she should be doing this, but she had to know what was going on in Chink's mind. She grabbed her wallet and her keys and headed out en route to the Hilton to finally put an end to her and Chink.

Fifteen minutes later, she was walking into the Hilton and up to the elevator to room 504. She had butterflies in her stomach as the elevator climbed floors. She slowly walked down the hall and noticed that the door was cracked open. She pushed the door in and noticed Chink sitting on the edge of the bed.

"Good to see you came." Chink spoke.

"Chink, what do you want with me?" Jonnae questioned.

"I just wanna talk to you Jonnae, that's all. And don't hit me with that two minute bullshit."

She rolled her eyes. "Talk then."

"Jonnae, do you love me?"

"What?"

"Just answer the question."

"Erick, I will probably always love you, but I can't be with you."

Chink got up and walked towards her, "Why?"

"Because all you do is hurt me, I deserve better than that."

He was now standing in front of her, "and that other nigga can treat you better than I did."

"He's been doing a damn good job."

Chink was now touching her, and Jonnae hated the fact that she was getting hot and bothered.

"Chink stop."

"Do you really want me too? If you can look me in my eyes right now and tell me to stop," he tilted her head to the side and kissed her neck, "I will."

Everything in her was screaming to run out the door, but her feet wouldn't move.

"You can't even say anything, can you?"

She looked dead at him, in his eyes, "Chink stop!"

She moved his hands off and headed for the door.

"Jonnae wait, I'm sorry. Let's just talk, please, give me ten minutes of your time."

Against her better judgment she stayed, "Talk."

When Jonnae arrived back at Boog's, neither Boog were Capo were there. It was well after two am. She constantly called both Boog and Capo's phones and both were going to voicemail.

"God, please let them be okay." No sooner than she opened her eyes from her prayer, she heard Capo's Corvette pull up. She ran to the door and as soon as Capo walked through the door, she jumped in his arms.

"I love you Ja'kahri."

"I love you too Jonnae."

Together they headed up to Boog's spare bedroom, laid down and passed out.

Epilogue

Things were calm over the next four weeks. Capo contacted the insurance company and they were moved into a condo with four bedrooms, three bathrooms, and just like the last home, Capo turned the basement into a movie theatre. Everything of value was taken from the old home and brought into the new home.

Lately, Jonnae had been feeling sick, but she didn't pay too much attention to it because it was normal to feel sick to her stomach when her period came around. She focused more on school since her senior year was coming to an end. After three straight days of throwing up everything, she finally decided to go to the drug store and grab a pregnancy test.

She was nervous as hell. She didn't want to be pregnant because she wasn't ready for kids. She went into the bathroom and squatted over the toilet to pee on the stick. She sat the test on the sink as she waited for the results. Capo opened the bathroom door and noticed the pink plus on the test. Jonnae started crying when she seen the positive results.

"I knew you were knocked up." Capo said. "Is it mine?"

Jonnae looked up at him like he had four heads, "excuse you?" She was taken aback.

"Jonnae don't lie to me. Is it mine?"

"Of course it is, why would..."

"Don't even try to play me. I followed you to the Hilton that night of the break-in. I found out it was Chink that was behind it. I also know it was Chink you went to see that night. You were there for more than two hours. So again, is it mine?

TO BE CONTINUED...

Excerpt from Hood Love 2

Prologue

Capo sat outside in his car and listened to the rain beat against the window pain as he smoked a blunt and thought about where he was at right now in his life. Jonnae hurt him bad; and it killed him thinking that the baby she was carrying may not be his. He thought back almost two months ago when he followed Jonnae from Boog's to the Hilton.

Capo had been feeling iffy ever since he asked Jonnae if she noticed anything about the intruders and she hesitated. That right there meant she knew something; something she didn't want to say. His gut was telling him that she was hiding something. When he went out the door, he and Boog both sat down the street from the house; just to kill the curiosity. Just as he suspected, Jonnae came walking out the house, jumped in her car and took off.

Fifteen minutes later, they pulled up to the Hilton. He watched Jonnae walk in the hotel and he sat outside waiting for her to come out. He suspected it was Chink who she came to meet because had it been anyone else, she wouldn't have come to a hotel to meet them. Boog noticed the look on Capo's face.

"Chill, bruh. We don't know who she came here to meet."

"You're right, we don't know, but we're about to find out. Do you know the niggas first and last name?"

Boog nodded, "Erick Jackson. You know, any nigga fuckin' with my sister, I gotta know everything about."

"Good, good; go inside and tell them you want to know if you're brother Erick Jackson is here. If they say yes, then that's who she's here with. "

Just the thought of it had Capo's blood boiling. He wanted to knock on every person's door until he found Jonnae. Boog got out the car and headed into the hotel. He walked up to the counter to the receptionist. He looked at her face and tried his hardest not to laugh. She looked to have five pounds of makeup caked on her face and it looked horrible. She was popping her gum so hard; her jaw looked like it was going to break. He shook his head.

"Excuse me; I'm looking to see if my brother is here?"

"What's his name?" she asked.

"Erick Jackson."

She typed in the name, "Yup, he's here. Room 504; do you want me to tell him that you're here?" she asked as she picked up the phone.

"Oh no, it's okay. I'm not staying; I just wanted to make sure he was safe. Thank you." Boog turned around and walked out the door back to the car.

He climbed in, "Bruh, he's in there."

Capo shook his head, he was pissed. He slouched lower in his chair.

"What you wanna do man?"

"I'm waiting here to see how long her ass is gonna stay. I know that's your sister man and if you don't wanna stay then I understand."

"This is your relationship bruh, I can't get her outta this one. Just don't do anything stupid, that's all I ask."

Capo nodded, "I got you, I just wanna see how long her ass is gonna stay here."

Boog called Kittie to pick him up. 'What are you doing Nae?' Boog thought to himself. Ten minutes later, Kittie pulled up. Boog dapped up Capo and jumped in the car with Kittie and pulled off.

"Let the waiting game begin." Capo said aloud. He pulled his fitted down over his eyes and waited. Two hours later, he watched her walk out, jump in her car and pull out.

"Two hours Jonnae? Fuck was you doing?" Capo asked to no one in particular. He headed back to Boog's house, taking the long way to give her time to get there.

Chapter 1 – Capo

Watching Jonnae walk into that hotel almost two months ago and come out two hours later, fucked my head up bad. Especially when I found out that Chink was there, it only made it worse. Jonnae cried and shouted that she didn't do anything with him and that they were just talking, but who do I look like, Boo Boo the fool? There's no way she could convince me that she didn't do shit with him. I mean not only did you meet a nigga at the hotel in the middle of the night, your ex at that?

When I noticed she was getting sick and shit, I knew she was pregnant. I knew it wasn't her period because when her periods coming, she throws up maybe once or twice. This time, she was throwing up every damn thing she ate.

I know, you're wondering why I waited four weeks right. In all honesty, I was hurt and scared to find out the truth. I didn't wanna believe that my Jonnae would do me dirty like that. I mean she knows everything I done been through with Vanessa's trifling ass and she turns around and does the same damn thing. So here I sit, in the driveway of the home that I used to share with Jonnae. I don't want to go inside because it's too quiet. I miss my shawty like crazy but I can't believe she did me like that.

The day we found out she was pregnant and I confronted

her about the hotel shit, I told her ass she had to go. It killed me to do it, but I couldn't stand to look at her. I felt like knocking the shit out of her, but I loved her little ass too much to do that to her. I hated seeing her cry the way she cried, but she betrayed me. She's been staying at Boog's; how do I know? Oh just because we on the outs, don't mean I don't still check on her. No matter what, I'm gonna love Jonnae til the death of me.

After smoking my second blunt, I finally decided to go in the house. I walked in, flicked on the light and my eyes instantly went straight to the picture of Jonnae and me sitting on the coffee table in the living room. I had to get out of this house; there are too many memories of her here. Since I told her she had to go that very night two months ago, I barely even stay here.

Looking at the picture, I was tempted to pick up the phone and call her. I just wanted to hear her soft voice. I shook my head, grabbed a change of clothes and headed back to the Marriott. Soon as I got to my suite, I pulled out my phone and sent Boog a text.

Me: How's my shawty?

Boog: She's straight man, but all she doin is crying – she keeps saying nothing happened && they was jus tlkin...

I sucked his teeth

Me: Boog, I wanna believe that my nigga, but ova 2 hours? idk man, shits sketchy ; damn I miss my baby

Boog: Y'all need to stop this! I love my sister but damn, this is too many emotions for me and she keep listening to these slow ass songs; I'm going crazy!

I laughed

Me: I dunno man, but good looks, I'll holla at you tomorrow!

Boog: Aight man, and hurry up and talk to this girl, she won't eat or nothing, regardless, that's my niece or nephew she's carrying so she betta get sum act rite or imma shove my foot in her ass!

Me: Lol aight man, I'm out.

I placed my phone on the charger and rolled over. "Sweet dreams mami, I love you." I closed my eyes, and tried to go to sleep.

Chapter 2 – Jonnae

I knew it was a bad idea going to meet Chink but my hard headed stubborn ass just had to go. Now look where I am; pregnant, depressed and staying with my brother. I barely drag my ass out the bed to go to school, but I'm at the end, too late to give up now. Plus, if Capo knew I didn't go to school, fuck being mad about Chink, he'd be ready to really lay my ass out.

God, I miss Capo. I tried calling and texting him; but he won't return any of my calls or texts. I've gone by the house but everything is still in the same place it's been in since the night of the argument; doesn't even look like he's been home. I wish he would believe me. Since he told me to leave, I've been at Boog's doing nothing but crying. I can't help but to cry, I know it looked bad, but I put it on my baby that we didn't do anything.

Here I am, laying in the bed listening to the rain outside. Its days like these when I miss Capo the most. On rainy days, we would lounge around the house being lazy together; watching movies, eating junk food and talking shit. Thinking about it brought tears to my eyes. I wish I could go back to that night and stick with my gut instinct and stay my ass right in the house. But no, I just had to go see what the fuck this nigga wanted.

As I was heading for the door, Chink stopped me, "Jonnae wait, I'm sorry. Let's just talk, please, give me ten minutes of your time."

I turned back towards him, walked over and sat in the chair, "talk."

"I just want you to know how truly and deeply sorry I am. For everything I have ever done, I am truly sorry. After I read your letter, I knew you were better off without me, but it's not easy letting go of the person you love."

"So Chink, if you really love me like you claim you do, why did you constantly hurt me? And then fuckin' Shakeisha for six months? Why?"

I felt myself getting choked up but I just had to know the answer.

"I'm a guy. I wanted my cake and I wanted to eat it too. It led me nowhere but losing the one I wanted the most. I took you for granted Nae, and I didn't realize it until you walked away from me. The whole Shakeisha thing, to keep it real, there is no reason. It was fucked up all around. She would always tell me that you complained about me and the shit I did and she wanted to see what the fuss was about. One thing led to another, and then there we were fucking. I hate that I ever did it. If I could take it back, I would but I can't, the damage is done."

I couldn't stop the tears that fell from my eyes knowing that my best friend wanted to fuck my man because I confided in her about how dirty he was doing me. Talk about loyalty.

"So why did you go over there the day after we broke up?"

He rubbed his hands over his face, "I was hurting and I needed something to get my mind off of everything. She was the easiest and closest."

I shook my head. Did this nigga really just say she was the easiest and the closest? I couldn't believe this shit.

"That day, I was actually going there to tell Shakeisha what happened and see what I should do as far as us. If I wanted to keep fighting for it to work or just let it go. Walking in on that gave me all the assurance I needed. Ending us what exactly what I needed to do." I told him.

"Jonnae, I can tell you until I'm blue in the face that I'm sorry but it won't change anything. I fucked up, I see that now and I'm telling you, if there was any way I could go back and fix it, I would change it. I won't lie, seeing that you moved on Is fuckin' with me bad ma. I never thought I would see this day. You moving on with the next nigga; I thought you'd forever be mine. But like I told you, all I want is for you to be happy, even if that means it's not with me. If this Capone dude is who you want, then who am I to intervene?"

"It's Capo," I corrected.

"Whatever the hell his name is."

I looked at him, "One more question, and then I gotta get running because I already been here for two hours when I said ten minutes."

"What's that?" he asked.

"Why did you break into our house?"

"Keeping it one hundred, I was hoping he was home alone. Then I could've shaken the nigga up a little or something and robbed him for some shit."

I shook my head, "And it's petty shit like that, that will keep us from ever being together again. I'm asking you Erick, please, don't call me anymore. I'm happy where I am, and I'd like to keep it that way."

I stood and walked out the door and headed back to my happiness.

I rolled over on my side and tried everything in my power not to cry. I was tired of crying. Pandora played softly from the iHome. I felt my phone vibrate and thought my eyes were playing tricks on me when I saw the message was from Capo.

Capo: Come open the door, I know you're up

I chuckled as I rolled outta bed and walked downstairs to get my baby out the rain. I was nervous, though. I hope he didn't come here to fight because I wasn't in the mood to do so. I opened the door and looked at him.

I gave him a small smile, "come on." I led him upstairs to the room I was in. I climbed back in the bed as he sat at the foot of the bed. We sat in awkward silent.

I had to break the silence, "How are you?"

He looked at me, "honestly, I'm hurting Nae."

"Capo, as bad as it looked, I put it on our unborn, we did nothing but talk. I promise."

I noticed him look at my stomach. "Why did you have to go? Why didn't you just tell me who it was when I asked ma?"

I sighed, "I had to know the reason why."

He chuckled, "you let your stubbornness get in the way. Sometimes, you gotta let me be the man Nae. Let me handle shit like that."

"I knew you would react first before finding out why."

"Because I don't give a fuck why!" he shouted. "The nigga shouldn't have broken into my shit. Why do I give a fuck about why the nigga did it?"

"Lower your voice nigga."

"Man fuck this shit, I came here to try and talk to you and you're sitting in my face taking up for the nigga."

"Ja'kahri, I'm not taking up for anybody but myself."

"So why justify the reason why you went?"

I had no come back. I shouldn't have gone, but curiosity and nosiness got the best of me.

"Exactly my point; I want a test on my shawty when it's born and I wanna know when your doctor's appointments are."

I screwed up my face, but I wasn't going to argue, "Fine, since my word ain't good enough, if a test is what you want, then a test is what you'll get."

He turned and began walking away but stopped to turn and say, "You better call the doctor tomorrow to set up an appointment. Don't try to be sneaky and not tell me shit. You hear me?"

I rolled my eyes, "As loud as you are, everyone and their fuckin' mama can hear your big ass mouth."

"Whatever!" With that, he turned and left. I didn't think he would come here and start an argument. I was hoping he was coming to tell me he wanted me to come home or to spend the night with me, but he ain't do shit but start a fucking argument about the same shit; again!

About The Author:

I'm Leondra LeRae and I'm an up and coming author out of Providence, Rhode Island. I have six siblings, a god son and a nephew. Since a child, I've enjoyed writing and always had a wild imagination. I enjoys writing in my free time as well as pursuing my dreams of becoming a doctor.

Feel free to contact and interact with me:
Email: authorleondralerae@gmail.com
Facebook (Personal): www.facebook.com/LeRaex3
Facebook (Fan/Like Page):
www.facebook.com/AuthorLeondraLeRae
Twitter: www.twitter.com/LeondraLeRae
Instagram: www.instagram.com/leo_xo

CPSIA information can be obtained
at www.ICGtesting.com
Printed in the USA
LVOW13s1559291116

514957LV00007B/655/P

9 781480 099692